TEMPLE OF THE JAGUAR

TEMPLE OF THE JAGUAR

A Nick Caine Adventure
#1

J.R. Rain
&
Aiden James

ACCLAIM FOR THE AUTHORS:

"Gripping, adventurous, and romantic—J.R. Rain's *The Lost Ark* is a breakneck thriller that traces the thread of history from Biblical stories to current-day headlines. Be prepared to lose sleep!"
—**James Rollins**, international bestselling author of *Bloodline*

"Aiden James has written a deeply psychological, gripping tale that keeps the readers hooked from page one."
—**Bookfinds** on *The Forgotten Eden*

"J.R. Rain delivers a blend of action and wit that always entertains. Quick with the one-liners, but his characters are fully fleshed out (even the undead ones) and you'll come back again and again."
—**Scott Nicholson**, bestselling author of *The Red Church*

"The intense writing style of Aiden James kept my eyes glued to the story and the pages seemed to fly by at warp speed. Twists, turns, and surprises pop up at random times to keep the reader off balance. It all blends together to create one of the best stories I have read all year."
—**Huntress Reviews** for *The Devil's Paradise*

OTHER BOOKS BY
J.R. RAIN

STANDALONE NOVELS
The Lost Ark
Elvis Has *Not* Left the Building
The Body Departed
Silent Echo
Winter Wind

SHORT STORY SINGLES
The Bleeder

VAMPIRE FOR HIRE
Moon Dance
Vampire Moon
American Vampire
Moon Child
Christmas Moon
Vampire Dawn
Vampire Games
Moon Island
Moon River
Vampire Sun
Moon Dragon

**SAMANTHA MOON
SHORT STORY COLLECTIONS**
Teeth and Other Stories
Vampire Nights and Other Stories

Vampires Blues and Other Stories
Vampire Dreams and Other Stories
Halloween Moon and Other Stories
Vampire Gold and Other Stories
Blue Moon and Other Stories
Dark Side of the Moon and Other Stories

JIM KNIGHTHORSE SERIES
Dark Horse
The Mummy Case
Hail Mary
Clean Slate
Night Run

JIM KNIGHTHORSE
SHORT STORY COLLECTIONS
Easy Rider and Other Stories

THE WITCHES TRILOGY
The Witch and the Gentleman
The Witch and the Englishman
The Witch and the Huntsman

THE SPINOZA TRILOGY
The Vampire With the Dragon Tattoo
The Vampire Who Played Dead
The Vampire in the Iron Mask

THE AVALON DUOLOGY
The Grail Quest
The Grail Knight

SHORT STORY COLLECTIONS
The Bleeder and Other Stories
The Santa Call and Other Stories
Vampire Rain and Other Stories

THE VAMPIRE DIARIES
Bound By Blood

SCREENPLAYS
Dark Quests

Co-Authored Books

COLLABORATIONS
Cursed! (with Scott Nicholson)
Ghost College (with Scott Nicholson)
The Vampire Club (with Scott Nicholson)
Dragon Assassin (with Piers Anthony)
Dolfin Tayle (with Piers Anthony)
Jack and the Giants (with Piers Anthony)
Judas Silver (with Elizabeth Basque)
Lost Eden (with Elizabeth Basque)
Deal With the Devil (with Elizabeth Basque)

NICK CAINE ADVENTURES
with Aiden James
Temple of the Jaguar
Treasure of the Deep
Pyramid of the Gods

THE ALADDIN TRILOGY
with Piers Anthony
Aladdin Relighted
Aladdin Sins Bad
Aladdin and the Flying Dutchman

THE WALKING PLAGUE TRILOGY
with Elizabeth Basque
Zombie Patrol
Zombie Rage
Zombie Mountain

OTHER BOOKS BY
J.R. RAIN

JUDAS CHRONICLES
Plague of Coins
Reign of Coins
Destiny of Coins
The Dragon Coin
Tyranny of Coins

DYING OF THE DARK SERIES
The Vampires' Last Lover
The Vampires' Birthright
Blood Princesses of the Vampires
Scarlet Legacy of the Vampires

NICK CAINE SERIES
Temple of the Jaguar (with J.R. Rain)
Treasure of the Deep (with J.R. Rain)
Pyramid of the Gods (with J.R. Rain)
Curse of the Druids

TALISMAN CHRONICLES
The Forgotten Eden
The Devil's Paradise
Hurakan's Chalice

Temple of the Jaguar

Copyright © 2012 by J.R. Rain and Aiden James

All rights reserved.

ISBN-10: 1501059513

ISBN-13: 9781501059513

DEDICATION

To Bartholomew, my friend and guide.
—J.R.

To my dearest Fiona, forever my love, my partner, and
my greatest muse. And, to J.R. Rain, whose friendship,
guidance, and steadfast support are beyond compare.
—Aiden

TEMPLE OF THE JAGUAR

"What I seek I find, what I find I keep."
—H. Rider Haggard, *King Solomon's Mines*

CHAPTER ONE

Ruinas, Honduras
Present Day

I found the ceremonial blade in the unmarked grave of some poor sap who had seen better days.

We'd been digging all day in this remote section of the rain forest, sweat pouring down our bare torsos, hands blistering despite the gloves. It was the golden reflection that first caught my eye—that wonderful golden flash that brings a smile to all of us who call ourselves looters. Although, I prefer the term 'creative archaeologists'.

I used the trowel to scrape away the remaining dirt, revealing more of the blade, which consisted of a jade hilt, an emerald capstone, and six inches of pure gold. And if I wasn't so tough, I could have cried right there.

"That will fetch a pretty penny," said Ishi from behind me in his native Tawankan tongue. Actually, in his native tongue, this was translated to mean that the knife could be exchanged for many shiny coins.

"Yes, Ishi," I said. "Many shiny coins."

I reached down between the ribs, plucked the knife by its hilt and hauled it out, letting the smattering of sunlight refract off its near-perfect finish. That drop of clear liquid on its golden blade was either a tear or sweat. Maybe I'm not so tough after all.

Ishi helped me out of the hip-deep grave, which I was only too glad to leave behind. Any grave robber worth his salt is always happy to leave a grave behind.

We sat back in the shade of a mangrove tree and I lit a cigarette and studied the knife, rolling it back and forth in the little sunlight that made its way to the jungle floor. The crimson glow of the cigarette tip reflected deeply within the blade. It was a rare find, indeed.

"He was a warrior," said Ishi, squatting next to me and drinking from a water jug. "Perhaps a very highly-esteemed warrior. The knife was for his protection."

I thought about that, then stood and moved over to the exposed grave. I unbuckled my pickaxe and dropped it down into the pit. I returned a moment later and sat down next to the Indian youth. "Can't leave the old chap without any protection."

Ishi was smiling. "You are not like the others."

"We all steal," I said, inhaling on the cigarette.

"But you steal with a conscience."

"I know. It's a terrible thing."

"At least you have not angered the spirits."

"Yes," I said, "there's always that. C'mon, let's re-bury this poor bastard and get the hell out of here."

———

As Ishi drove through the thick jungle on a road that really wasn't much of a road, I checked my voice mail on my looting hotline. One new message. Oh, fun. It was from a woman named Marie Da Vinci. She wanted to speak with me ASAP. Unless my ass was on the line, I rarely did anything ASAP, which is one of the reasons I became a self-employed looter. It was either that or open a smoothie shop in a strip mall.

I listened to the message again. The voice was strong but firm, breathy and sexy. She wanted to meet me today at four, in the outdoor cafe at the Copan Rio Hotel, of which I happened to live on the fifth floor.

After a moment's contemplation, I dialed the number. It rang twice, and then went straight to voice mail. I heard the same sultry voice. I left a message: I would meet her at the hotel restaurant at four. I clicked off the phone.

"Hot date?" asked Ishi. Actually, this was translated to mean: a formal assembly between two possible mates for the continuation of one's paternal bloodline.

"Yeah," I said, "something like that."

"Does she know you're a thief?"

"She called me on my looting hotline," I said. "So I'm thinking yes."

Ishi smiled and said to himself, "Looting hotline. Shit."

I leaned back in the front seat, closed my eyes and listened to the slapping of branches against the hood and fenders, the call of the distant howler monkeys, the chirping of hundreds of tropical birds.

Breathy and sexy? Oh boy.

CHAPTER TWO

Juan Esteban examined the knife closely, making excitable little noises that didn't seem all that appropriate for the circumstances.

He was using a jeweler's glass, examining every inch of the artifact, and making notes on a small pad. Then he placed the knife carefully on a white cloth and moved over to his logs, pulling one from his shelf and flipping through the pages.

We were alone in his shop. The shop itself was in Coco, a little town north of the Copan ruins. For all intents and purposes, Juan's shop looked like a run-down pawnshop. There were a half dozen glass cases cluttering the store, most of them with broken doors, filled with very cheap watches and fake jewelry and rusted pistols from Honduras's colonial days. I moved around the shop and examined a rifle that actually appeared to be bent, completely useless.

This wasn't exactly the famous "black market" people hear about, but Juan usually unloads any of the jewelry or specialty items I may find. The golden dagger would be considered a specialty item.

"You sell junk," I told him again.

"Of course. It keeps the thieves and policia away, although sometimes they are one in the same."

I pointed to the bent rifle. "Have you ever sold any of this crap?"

He chuckled. "Last week a tourist came by. She liked a plastic ring. I told her it was folk art." He snapped shut his ledger, came back and sat behind his desk. "I've only seen one other dagger like this. Appears to be from the Mayan post-preclassic. Ceremonial. Never used for actual battle, of course. A jade hilt and an emerald capstone, and although the gold is low-grade, like most Mayan gold, it is a very rare find and very valuable indeed."

"I'm surprised, Juan. You're not up to your old tricks. By now you've usually told me how worthless an artifact is."

"You've caught me on an off day, and I've never been able to take advantage of you, Nick, so I've given up trying."

"Very admirable of you to admit, Juan. But we both know that's bullshit. What are you offering?"

"Two thousand."

"American dollars?"

"Of course."

I laughed appropriately. "Fifty thousand dollars, and not a penny less."

He sat back, shocked. "You would extort from a friend, my friend?"

"You were never much of a friend."

"Now you insult me. Well, I spit on your mother's grave, goddammit."

I laughed at his showmanship and scooped up the knife. "My mother is alive and well, I think. Maybe I'm not ready to sell just yet. It is, after all, quite beautiful. Maybe it's also good luck."

"Ten thousand, and that's my final offer."

"I don't think so. You'll get ten times that from the New York collectors. Call me with a decent offer. Good day."

"Twenty thousand and consider it a gift."

"Adios, amigo."

I left his shop and stepped out onto the empty dirt street. Ishi was sitting in the Jeep with the windows down and his Panama hat pulled over his eyes. He was out like a light. As soon as I opened the door he snapped awake.

"Well?" he asked, pushing up his hat.

"We'll hear from him soon enough."

"What did he offer?"

"Twenty Gs."

Ishi whistled. "I would have taken it."

"We can get more. A lot more."

"Which is why you do the negotiating."

"Yes," I said.

"So what good am I?" he asked.

"You're here for entertainment purposes."

"Good to know."

"Drive on, Ishi. Let's get out of here. I have a date."

He shifted gears, and we left the small town in a cloud of dust.

CHAPTER THREE

"Nick Caine?"

I nodded and smiled. Ever the approachable stranger.

Marie Da Vinci was a pretty woman with an angular face and muscular arms. Probably spent five to six days a week with a personal trainer. There were wet splotches under her breasts; a film of sweat coated her forehead and forearms. Sub-tropical humidity has that effect. She unconsciously pulled her sticky shirt away from her skin and grimaced, as if sweating through her clothes was distasteful.

She looked good, distasteful and all.

Having sworn off all women years ago, I was concerned by my immediate attraction to her. I thought: *watch yourself, Nick Caine, Looter Extraordinaire.*

I was sitting in an outdoor cafe along the dirt streets of Ruinas, Honduras, just outside the Hotel Rio Copan. Drinking beer from the bottle. Or, as the song says, just wasting away.

"Thank you for meeting me on such short notice," she said.

"Luckily, you caught me before my power nap," I said.

She smiled. "May I sit?"

"Suit yourself." Ever the courteous gentleman, I kicked out one of the whicker chairs opposite me. It skidded to a stop next to her feet. She brushed the chair with a paper napkin, and then sat on said napkin. The chair promptly creaked whicker-like. The alert Honduran waiter swooped in and asked in broken English if she would like a drink. He assumed correctly that she was both thirsty and a tourist. The copious amounts of sunscreen on her narrow nose and the bright pink blouse were the dead giveaways. In this humidity, the thirst was a given, of course.

"A glass of water please," she said.

The waiter blinked, then looked at me. I shrugged at the waiter. The waiter waited. Marie looked at the waiter, then me and said, "What's wrong?"

"Ordering a glass of water is a bad idea," I said.

She nodded, blushed. "Of course. A *bottle* of water, please."

"Of course, senorita."

An old Miskito woman stood under an umbrella at the nearby street corner, encouraging all within earshot to try her amazing lemonade. I had tried it earlier. It was amazing.

I said to Marie, "There's a man out here named Da Vinci. Leonardo Da Vinci. And from what I understand he's a shitty artist, which, I suppose, is kind of ironic."

At the mention of Leonardo Da Vinci she looked away. Her lower lip might have trembled, too. I continued, "He is, however, a murderous looting kingpin who would just as soon cut your throat open than lend you a dime. Rumor has it that he's making a big move into the drug business." I paused, studying her reaction. "No offense, but you wouldn't happen to be related?"

There was no hesitation. "He's my uncle."

"Ah."

The old lady on the corner raised her voice even louder, shouting in English, Spanish, Miskito and a mixture of all three. Hell, I even detected some French. Finally, she stepped out from under her yellow umbrella and out into the heat of the sun. Like a lioness picking off the weak and sick from the herd, she picked out a young man from a milling crowd and guided him toward her lemonade stand. The young man looked confused and a little scared. I didn't blame him. She thrust a waxy cup full of the good stuff and practically reached down into his trousers for his money. He thanked her but looked thoroughly shaken when he retreated to his pack.

Marie continued, "He killed my father. His own goddamned flesh and blood."

She pulled out a tissue and dabbed her eyes carefully. Her eyes were round, like Japanese anime, and I noticed for the first time the faintish, darkish, puffy circles under them, like twin-blackened moons in their quarter phase. When done dabbing, she crumpled the tissue and held it in her fist, should there be later tears. Recycling in action, folks.

"I'm sorry," I said.

"You don't seem surprised."

"Your uncle, Miss Da Vinci, is a cold-hearted killer. And not a very nice man," I said. "However, killing his own brother seems to be a new low for Leo."

"You seem to know him."

"Let's just say we've had reason to cross paths. Your uncle doesn't like competition, and his competition has a habit of disappearing."

"But you're still alive."

"No small feat. If it was up to your uncle, I'd be dead by now."

She studied me carefully, and seemed to reappraise, looking me over like a used car. Maybe if I were lucky she'd kick my tires.

"Your father owned a museum in California," I said, prodding.

"You know of my father?"

I grinned. "I'm just full of surprises."

"Well, the museum was burned to the ground," she said. "Everything was lost. My father's entire legacy, destroyed."

"I assume Uncle Leo had a hand in that as well."

"Yes."

She seemed about to tell me more but her drink came. She opened the bottle with a deft twist and took a long pull and wiped the corners of her mouth with her thumb and forefinger. Her hand was shaking. She twisted the cap back on and set the bottle on the wooden table. Next, she removed a small notepad from her purse, flipped to a page and looked at me steadily. Her blue eyes were flecked with gold. My favorite color.

11

She looked down at the pad. "You, of course, are a looter."

"I prefer the term *creative archaeologist*," I said and reached over and tilted down her notepad with my forefinger. There was much scribbling on the page, with my name written on top, underlined twice. Hmmmm. "Where did you get this?," I asked. "I'm not exactly listed in the yellow pages under Looting."

She grinned. "I'm full of surprises as well, Mr. Caine. As it turns out, you are fairly well-known in the museum industry. A looter who's not entirely untrustworthy."

"Mom would be proud."

She went back to the notepad. "You have a Ph.D in Classical Mayan socio-economics from UCLA."

"Sounded good at the time. But just try getting a job at Microsoft."

"You worked briefly as an acquisitions specialist for the Bowers Museum of Cultural History in Santa Ana, California. Your last official job."

"Yes."

"But you quit."

I shrugged. "As it turns out, I had quite a knack for acquiring artifacts, and an even stronger desire to keep them for myself."

She closed the notebook, put it back in her purse. I knew there was still more information in there about me. Curiosity killed the looter.

"So," I said, "did I pass the test?"

She looked at me with those big round eyes. The circles seemed to be getting darker. She needed sleep. Probably a couple days' worth. "Yes, I suppose you did," she said.

"Oh, swell. Now it's your turn. What's this all about?"

CHAPTER FOUR

She sat back and crossed her legs. Her ankles were tan. Tan ankles did something to me. Her foot bounced as she spoke. "You are, of course, familiar with the legends surrounding Ciudad Blanca."

I sat back. "It's a fairy tale."

"It's *not* a fairy tale, Mr. Caine."

"Oh? You've been there? What's it like?"

She smiled and reached out and touched the back of my hand. I once heard that a good salesperson would always touch their mark. I felt like a mark. As if I were being manipulated through a sales pitch. Except that I liked her pitch—and her touch.

Oh, brother.

The waiter came by and looked at me. I shook my head and he went away. Meanwhile, she watched me carefully, perhaps trying to gauge my reaction. The flecks in her eyes glittered like fool's gold. Except, I was beginning to feel like the fool. She slipped something into my hand.

"What's this?" I asked.

"Look at it."

I did. It was a Polaroid of a limestone disc and a rotund older man standing next to it, smiling as if he were with a lover. The disc was taller than his hip, larger than the ones I had come across. I squinted, and was able to pick out one or two familiar glyphs, which seemed to speak of rivers and valleys. The majority of the text, however, was unknown to me. The glyphs spiraled out from the center for three rows in what could only be a very complex story. Or a complex set of directions. The text encircled an image of a stylized jaguar, a popular image in Mayan lore. I was intrigued by the size of the jaguar, easily twice as big as a man. "It's a photograph of a Mayan disc glyph."

"Ancient directions to Ciudad Blanca," she said. "It's why my father was killed."

I noticed she wasn't wearing a wedding band, and knew immediately that I shouldn't care if she was wearing one or not. But I did, and the warning bells continued to sound in my head.

"My father found the disc on an excavation in the Copan valley thirty years ago. He returned it to the museum, where he has been deciphering it ever since. *Had* been deciphering it." She looked away, pained.

"Has the entire text been deciphered?"

She nodded. "Finished on the night he was murdered."

"Coincidence?"

"No," she said. "My uncle, you see, had a sort of spy working in the museum. Apparently, this bastard had been reporting on my father's progress. My uncle waited thirty years for the glyph to be deciphered."

"How do you know this?"

"He told me."

"When?"

"Right after the funeral. He and I had a sort of family reunion." She reached into her purse and pulled out a clear CD ROM case. "He was looking for this."

I reached for it, but she held it back.

"What's on it?" I asked.

"The deciphered disc glyph in its entirety. A road map that goes through the jungles of Honduras. And, it goes on to Ciudad Blanca." She paused. "Uncle Leo managed to steal everything but the final clue to Ciudad Blanca, a clue contained on this

16

disk. The final clue my father deciphered on the night he was murdered."

"And how did you manage to get the disk?"

"Father emailed me the results as a precaution. He correctly suspected he was being watched. I had the information burned to a disk."

"So, Uncle Leo has everything but the final location of Ciudad Blanca."

She nodded. "He can start, but he can't finish."

I smiled and sat back. "I hate when that happens."

CHAPTER FIVE

Wwe were in my looting command center, on the fifth floor of the Hotel del Rio.

The suite was cluttered with enough relics to fill a small museum, or two, all piled on dozens upon dozens of bookshelves. Most artifacts were of Mayan and Olmec origin: flint knives, beads, pottery, carved figurines, statuettes, carved reliefs and jewelry. I even had two life-sized obsidian skulls. Virtually priceless. I had boxes filled with spear points and tools and utensils, all labeled accordingly, and all piled around the entire suite.

"You are a busy little looter," she said, stepping inside behind me. She went straight to the flint knives, as most do. Ornate jade carvings with razor edges. She touched the fine edge tentatively.

"The artifacts are there for the taking. I catalogue all my finds as well or better than most archaeologists, and I only sell to respectable museums. All on the hush-hush, of course, as most museums have an official policy to not negotiate with known looters. But, privately, I've had scores of representatives from many famous museums peruse these very shelves."

She put her hands over her ears. "I don't want to know any more."

I grinned. "True, it's a dirty little secret. In fact, I've sold to your father's museum countless times, although I did not deal with him directly."

She dropped her hands and sighed. "Father was obsessed only with his disk glyph—and left the day to day running of the museum to myself and others."

She set the flint knife down and removed a manila file folder from her over-sized purse. She flipped it open and handed me two copies of a computer printout.

"What's this?" I asked.

"It's the partially printed text from the disc glyph."

"Partially?"

She smiled sweetly. "It's for my protection, Mr. Caine."

"Ah," I said. "You still don't trust me."

"If you were in my position, would you?"

"Point taken," I said, scanning the pages. "What do you want from me, Miss Da Vinci?"

"I need someone who knows the land. Someone who can follow these ancient directions." As she spoke she circled around me. She put a hand on my shoulder. The final sales pitch. "My father had in his notes that you were that man. And from what I've seen and heard, you will more than do."

I shrugged my shoulders and stepped away from her. I did not like the way my heart skipped a beat at her touch. I was serious about not getting involved with another woman—especially after what happened last time.

I said, "At some point you will have to furnish the rest of the document, Miss Da Vinci. At some point you will have to trust me."

She crossed her arms over her chest; her soft lips grew much harder. "Once we agree to be partners I will furnish the remaining documents. But trust is another matter, Mr. Caine. Trust must be earned."

"Does your lack of trust have something to do with my occupation?"

"You are a looter and a thief. It has everything to do with your occupation, Mr. Caine."

CHAPTER SIX

Looters get a bad wrap. Just because we steal and plunder and operate outside of the law doesn't mean we're all bad guys.

We spent the remaining night going over the first two pages of the translation. The trail began at a river whose Mayan name never changed, which was lucky for us. From there things got a little tricky, but I was relatively certain I knew of the route, although the names for some rivers had changed. One thing was clear: the route led into the heart of La Mosquita. The Mosquita Coast. Little Amazon. Some of the last unexplored terrain on earth.

The rivers were accurate, their lengths and widths described were accurate enough, too. Whether or not this map led to Ciudad Blanca remained to be seen.

One thing was for certain…the path seemed to lead into the mountains. Not through…*into*.

"We'll be traveling through tunnels," I said.

Marie clapped her hands. "I just love a good adventure story."

"Oh. You have many?"

Still grinning, she looked at me. "No, this will be my first."

I rolled my eyes. Had Ishi been here, he would have rolled his eyes, too. Looters didn't have much use for amateurs. Amateurs tended to get in the way…and to get killed.

Anyway, Marie seemed quite pleased with my grasp of the map's instructions. She had feared, she said, that the directions would make little sense, even to an experienced guide like myself, and that her father's life work had been for not.

"So, Mr. Caine, will you guide me into the jungle?"

"One condition?"

"What's that?"

"Quit calling me Mr. Caine."

Actually, there was a second condition. We looters always have a second condition. Next, we discussed my guiding fees, and when we were both satisfied, we agreed to meet tomorrow to coordinate the expedition. She gathered her stuff and made a beeline to my door. I was beelining right behind her.

"What do you plan on doing once you get there?" I asked.

She spoke over her shoulder. "Where?"

"Ciudad Blanca?"

"Conduct a full excavation," she said. "With much of the artifacts going to a bigger and better museum, built in my father's honor."

"And what of the supposed treasure?" I asked.

She turned and faced me. Her eyes touched upon different features of my face. "Why there will be no treasure...Nicholas."

"Nick," I said. "Oh, really?"

"Not after we split it."

I grinned. "You would make a hell of a looter."

"I suspect most of us would, when it comes right down to it."

"And what if your uncle happens upon the city?"

She set her jaw. "I have plans for my uncle. Now, good night, Nick. I will see you tomorrow."

She left. I watched her go and when she disappeared down a stairwell, I shut my door and leaned against it, wondering what the hell I had gotten myself into.

CHAPTER SEVEN

I t was late.

The city had long ago shut down, and the hotel I lived in had long ago settled in for the night. Fuego wasn't known for its nightlife, which was fine by me. I was sitting in a lawn chair on my balcony overlooking the city. There was no lawn, but I often thought of myself as a maverick. In the distance, Lake Huron glimmered under the moonlight. The rest of the city didn't glimmer much, although a few lights twinkled here and there. More mavericks.

Smoke from my hand-rolled cigarette curled up before my eyes. The smoke stung but I didn't show it. Partly because I was growing more and more numb with each inhalation, each lungful of smoke. Partly because this wasn't exactly a cigarette.

I inhaled deeply. The tip of the cheroot flared briefly, the paper casing crackling and sizzling. At least, I think it crackled and sizzled. This was my second smoke, and anything was possible at this point.

Case in point, the image of a man in my peripheral vision. When I turned my head, he was gone. Or, rather, just managed to slip out of my field of vision. There he was now, apparently lounging against the iron railing, watching me get wasted again. I turned my head quickly, hoping to catch him, but he was gone, baby, gone.

My eyes settled on the near distance. The city lights were blurring. I momentarily puzzled over the two moons. Until I realized one of the moons was a reflection in the water. This took me about two minutes to figure out. The little man appeared again, watching me from the railing. I think he was smiling. It was hard to tell. I turned my head. He was gone, gliding just out of my field of vision.

I had to urinate. So I did. Off my balcony. At least I think I did. When I sat back down, I wasn't sure why the hell I had gone over the balcony in the first place.

I sucked some more on the cheroot and images of my parents flooded my mind. I saw them smiling and happy. Working together in the field. A true team. My father jotting down notes as my mother carefully analyzed a clay pot. She turned the pot carefully in her hand, her trained eye seeing everything. My father was nodding and writing quickly. This was how they often worked. Two minds working as one. My mother was beautiful. Hard but beautiful. Her arms were more defined than my father's. In fact, I often suspected that my own muscle tone was inherited from my mother, rather than my father. Then again, I didn't look anything like my father, so who knew. Maybe there was a UPS driver out there who had gotten lucky one afternoon.

My eyes were watering from the smoke. At least, I think they were watering. I wiped the tears away and moved the burning tip away from my face.

They were nearly cut in two by the machine gun fire. I had been sleeping. We lived in a small house at the edge of town. This was their home base. They worked long hours from this house, in-between fieldwork and lectures. I had my own room in the back, which was where I had been when I heard the truck pull up, followed by some shouting. And as I lay there in the dark, I heard the machine gun fire. And the screams. And the laughter. And more tires squealing. And then silence.

I had waited perhaps ten minutes for my mother to come in and tell me everything was all right. She never did. And what I found outside was so horrible. So damned horrible.

I took another hit, and held the smoke in my lungs and noticed that everything around me was wavering and blurry. The man in my peripheral was gone. He was replaced by a red balloon. But when I turned my head, much slower this time, the balloon was blown off course, just out of my field of vision.

My parents were reduced to slaughtered meat, barely recognizable. No child should have to endure this.

A cool breeze came off the lake. I was sweating. The breeze felt good.

The red balloon drifted up and up, and I watched it go, or tried to watch it go, and then I fell over in my chair, and that's where I found myself the next morning, covered in ashes, a burn mark on my cheek.

My parents would have been proud.

CHAPTER EIGHT

"**A**re you sure you're up for this?"

It was a question delivered with more irritation than compassion. Ms. Da Vinci had arrived the next morning, just after sunrise. She stared worriedly at the red welt upon my right cheek. The devilish, dimpled smile I also inherited from my mom did little to minimize that fact, as well as the redness in my eyes. But, hell, at least I had showered and shaved.

"I'm fine," I told her, and then nodded approvingly at the vehicle she brought for our trip. A late model Jeep with the rental company proudly displayed on the back bumper. "Are you sure you can handle this thing? I hear they tip over pretty easily."

"It has a wider wheelbase than what you're thinking of…. But, if it's my driving that you're worried about, I'll let you drive."

She eyed me smugly, making her all the more alluring. Dressed in khakis with her sunglasses perched atop her head, she could pass for a typical tourist…except for those magical eyes of hers. I tried not to think long on any of it. Just give her a few hours and the humidity should melt away some of the charm.

"No, that is *my* job!"

"Well, I'll be damned…you made it on time!" I said, as Ishi ran up to us. He was carrying a large backpack upon his shoulders. "I see that you remembered the hand picks and trench shovels. Good man."

"Who the hell is he?"

"My right hand man," I said, dishing out a little of my own smugness. "Ishi, I'd like you to meet the nice lady I told you about last night: Ms. Marie Da Vinci."

"It's a pleasure to meet you…" Ishi's wide smile died as she huffed and moved over to the Jeep.

"This wasn't part of the deal, but we haven't got all day to discuss this," she said, opening the back of the vehicle. "Throw your shit in here, and let's get going."

She stomped toward the front of the Jeep and climbed in the driver's seat, immediately starting up the engine.

"I guess it ain't your job today," I told Ishi, grinning wryly. "For now, you had better leave the talking to me."

He scowled, but nodded in agreement. We hurried to climb into the Jeep before our irritated client laid on the horn.

I cut Ishi a wry grin as we hurried to get into the Jeep

"Doesn't look like you'll be driving," I said to my friend.

When normally in a rush I wouldn't bother taking a shower. Hell, once we were in the jungle's heat it wouldn't matter anyway. But, for some damned reason I felt I should be as gentlemanly as four minutes would allow. It was just enough to take a cold shower and gargle away the lingering gin from the night before.

Rather than give me any more clues as to what she knew about the disk and the road to Ciudad Blanca, Marie deftly turned the conversation to lighter subjects. That surprised me. Not the subjects themselves, but rather the fact we were soon discussing the Jeep she had rented for us the next day, and a week's supplies. She didn't like my joke about getting lost in an unexplored jungle and fighting over the last strip of jerky and a bottle of water before one of us turned into Alfred Packer.

It was an out-of-sync feeling for Ishi and I, since normally its just him and me traveling together to a site. And, it's not like we hadn't made a trip before into the hostile jungles surrounding the remains of Ciudad Blanca. Hell, the entire area has been picked over since Cortes failed to find the legendary city and its immense caches of gold and precious gems—not to mention other artifacts that many a museum would pay a handsome fee for.

I prepared to give Marie some well-deserved grief about wasting our time looking for something that was likely no longer there. But her intuitions beat me to the punch.

"You're probably thinking we're headed for the city wall structures that have recently been uncovered. Right?" she said, wearing a smirk not all that unlike the one I had been wearing since we veered from the main highway twenty minutes earlier.

"Ain't that where we're headed?" I snickered softly, and Ishi echoed that sentiment loud enough to draw an angry glance from our present employer.

"Hmmmm. You'll see in a moment."

She suddenly swung the Jeep onto a rutted dirt road that veered away from the excavated walls she mentioned. In fact, there really wasn't much of a road at all...just a worn truck path through the thick brush and mostly undisturbed vegetation. This would really suck if she hit an unseen boulder or tire-rut that could snap the bouncing vehicle's front axle.

But just when the bounces threatened to catapult Ishi from his seat and out into the surrounding mangroves, Marie veered onto yet another old road. This one, however, wasn't anywhere near as difficult to navigate through. Marie rolled down her window while slowing the vehicle down to where it crept along the road. The jungle trees and other plant life had been cleared here long ago, although the mangroves and vines had made a concerted effort to encroach upon the beaten path as it led deeper into the jungle.

"I don't suppose there's a Howard Johnson's up ahead," I deadpanned. "According to every legend, map, or drunken Meskito I've dealt with since I've been down here, there ain't nothin' worth the pain in the ass it can turn into out here. In fact, most Hondurans will tell you there isn't anything out here, period. So, you better not be lost."

"I'm not lost," she said, eying me coyly. I felt like a heel for being an ass a moment ago, and the way her lovely eyes regarded me…"We're less than a mile from where that photograph of my father was taken. We'll need to park and walk in a moment."

Maybe it was the cool comfort inside the Jeep. But she seemed much more in control of herself as compared to the night before. Of course, that would likely change in a few minutes, when the oppressive heat was re-introduced to our lovely companion. Especially considering that the road had a significant incline. Soon she and we would be covered in sweat and dust…I tried not to think what that combination would look like on her if she were naked. But, it sure beat the hell out of thinking of Ishi sans his clothes.

When Marie decided to park, it was damned near as abrupt as when she entered this God-forsaken side-road. She wasn't in the mood for idle chit-chat, which made me think maybe she'd be all right in the humid heat that would make her clothes cling to her sumptuous curves. Good for me, and a nice distraction to look forward to. As for the destination she sought…well it wasn't as close as she said it'd be, since she took off looking for it before Ishi and I had exited the Jeep.

"The place will still be there in five minutes," I chided her, to little avail, and even less of a reply. She headed up the hill to what looked like a small cave opening that was partially hidden in dense foliage.

"Why is she so much like a zombie?" asked Ishi. In truth, he likely meant to say a different word. Then again, she was acting like something foreign had taken over her brain.

"Just take it as the difference between an American and Honduran female," I said, hoping he'd follow my lead to run after her.

"I heard that!"

She glanced over her shoulder, but didn't stop until she had reached a flat boulder resting against another almost twice its size, a few feet away from the cave's entrance. She waited for Ishi and me to catch up to her.

"This is the spot where my father had his picture taken with the Jaguar disk," she said, her tone suddenly sad as if reminiscing about that moment. "It was right after his crew drug it out from below the earth."

"Drug it out with what?" I moved over to the cave. It seemed much deeper than it had from when I first noticed it. Something slithered amid the vines that threatened to obscure the cave entrance someday soon. "From inside here?"

Ishi joined me while looking around warily. Most critters guarding an entrance like this one are either venomous or aggressive, and usually both.

"Yes, and that's where we'll need to go next," she said, smiling smugly.

There was a private joke in there somewhere…and it wouldn't be about the fact her damp clothing hugged her curves.

Ishi began separating the vines around the cave entrance—and nearly did a back flip when a pair of bats flew up out of the hole. He must've startled them awake. Marie chuckled.

I scowled at her and came up behind Ishi. Among other things, I keep a small, high-powered flashlight at my hip. I'll leave the torches for Indiana Jones, thank you. I snapped it on and flashed it through the opening. There was, I could see, a formidable pit just inside the entrance—a pit that had been nearly covered in a tangle of vines. And not just any pit. It seemed to span from cave wall to cave wall, with no apparent way around it. No doubt many an adventurer had met his fate at whatever lay at the bottom of the pit. Too far to jump. I aimed the light higher…nothing but darkness.

I stepped back and turned to my friend.

"Ishi, get the ropes—"

"You won't need a rope or a vine to get down there," she chided.

"How do you know?"

"I'll show you," she said, and moved around me, and pushed through the tangle of vines…and promptly disappeared.

CHAPTER NINE

I shi looked at me, raising his eyebrows. But I was already moving, sweeping aside the hanging vines and stepping over a particularly nasty-looking banana spider, when a voice called out from the dark depths of the cave.

"Careful, Nick."

I was now standing at the edge of the pit, perhaps closer than I had intended. Indeed, rocks and debris spilled over, falling for many, many seconds before I heard muffled clattering from far below. Deep pit. I hate that.

I flashed my light over the darkened cave walls, scattering shadows and critters alike, until I found a peculiar sight. It was Marie and, not unlike the other critters scurrying before the light, was crawling along the wall herself.

"What in the hell?"

Ishi came up behind me, brushing me slightly, knocking me forward just enough where I nearly lost my lunch as I reached back and caught the tail of his shirt, stabilizing myself.

Ishi mumbled an apology—perhaps a little too halfheartedly for my tastes—and must have spotted Marie on the wall. Not hard to miss since she was presently the focus of my single beam of light. The Tawankan mumbled something about a devil monkey, which I, in a rare burst of good taste, decided not to relay.

"There're...handholds...to your right," she gasped, leaping from the wall and landing safely at the far end of the sizable pit, where just enough ambient light from the tunnels entrance illuminated her way.

"Hand—what?"

She turned on her own flashlight and pointed to her left, my right. I looked, following her finger, flashing my light over the walls. I didn't see it at first—in fact, not until Ishi ran his hand over the wall and gripped something that looked remarkably like a handhold, although perfectly camouflaged within the wall.

Ishi pointed and I spied a trail of such handholds and foot ledges that led around the pit, to the far side, where Marie presently stood, hands on hips and grinning.

"How in the hell did you know—" And then it occurred to me. "The disc glyph," I said, nodding.

"But of course. Now come on. You're wasting time!"

Ishi was already moving, gripping the handholds and stepping up onto a barely discernible ledge. Soon the native Tawankan was moving hand over hand, stepping from ledge to ledge, like a devil monkey himself. Myself, I didn't move as quickly or as confidently, and as I gripped each subsequent stone protrusion, I recalled her father's notes from the night before. They had indeed spoken of the spider's path over the well of souls. At the time, we had no clue what it referenced.

But Marie had put it all together—and quickly. Even putting her life at risk in the process. That bespoke of her confidence in herself. Or her foolishness. And in the looting game, both could get you killed.

Now, as I dropped to the dust-covered tunnel floor—fairly confident that the nail to my right index finger had split down the middle, I caught Ishi's wide-eyed expression, and I knew he was equally impressed.

"Don't look so surprised, Mr. Caine. I am, after all, my father's daughter. Now c'mon, according to my father's directions we're supposed to look for a river."

And with that, she turned and headed deeper into the tunnel, confidently sweeping her light before her.

Or foolishly. Either way, Ishi and I soon followed.

———

Most subterranean tunnels tend to get warmer the deeper one goes, and this one was no different. Soon we were all sweating through our shirts. Some of us more profusely than others.

"She sweats a lot for a woman," said Ishi in his native tongue.

"I noticed," I said.

"Not that I'm complaining," he added.

"Neither am I."

Marie looked back at us and raised an eyebrow, but I couldn't help but detect a small smirk on her face. Or maybe it was a trick of lighting.

The tunnel wasn't much of a tunnel. It seemed more like a series of descending platforms that led deeper and deeper into the earth. To where, I hadn't a clue, but I suspected a river might very well be in our immediate future. Especially since her father was considered one of the world's foremost experts on Pre-Columbian Mesoamerican paleo-linguistics, and the map translation Marie had shown to me last night spoke an underground river.

That, and he nailed the spider-thing around the Pit to Hell, or whatever it was called.

Her father was a man I both trusted and respected. A man who was now dead, thanks to his own brother. I shook my head, reminding myself to stay far away from the Da Vinci family reunions.

We reached a section of tunnel that was nearly a twenty-foot drop. I went first, despite Marie's protests. I was going to have to keep an eye on her. Her need to prove herself was going to get her hurt. Or dead.

A good thing, too. As I dropped down, landing lightly on a small shelf of rock, I wasn't entirely prepared for what I came face to face with.

CHAPTER TEN

"**W**hat do you see down there?"

"Shhh!" I scolded Ishi, as I glanced at where he crouched above me. "Unless you want me to become dinner for this thing."

Dinner? More like a cheap 'bar and grill' appetizer.

It might've been a snake. Or, perhaps some sort of prehistoric eel that had managed to outwit thousands of years of evolution by hiding in the depths of this god-forsaken place. Maybe that's why Cortes never found the gold he sought. Maybe it's also why very few explorers—namely none not named Da Vinci— even know about this cave system that I'd never heard of before. Maybe it's—

"What in the hell is holding us up, Nick?"

Count on the diva in the band to be thinking only of her pretty neck and self-imposed deadlines.

"It might take a moment to figure this out."

Hopefully, anyway. It all depended on what the thing eyeballing me from less than three feet away decided to do first. It eyed me emotionlessly as it hung down from a deep-growing tree root. The flashlight's beam might've eventually caught the damned thing, but I had immediately noticed the glowing lines along the sucker's back and legs. Its cold eyes were aglow, resembling two perfect moons. In fact, the only things not glowing on this bioluminescent critter were its teeth. I might not have ever seen them if they hadn't suddenly been revealed in the narrow halogen beam.

"Figure what out? We haven't got all goddamned day, Nick!"

"Then maybe you'd like to come down here and say hello to our new friend."

I didn't wait for her reply. I couldn't. Did I mention that this lizard thing, which sort of looked like a cross between a giant eel, snake, and gila monster had suddenly dropped down onto a narrow ledge ahead of me? Probably not. I imagine I likely also forgot to mention that its bared teeth were nearly as long as my fingers, and I know for damned sure I never told anyone that these teeth had green slime dripping down them as the critter salivated. If it was preparing for a meal, then I was more likely the entrée as opposed to a dinner guest.

"We're coming down, Nick!" Ishi advised.

"No!"

"What?!" said our princess. "You obviously need our help, so here we—*Oh my God, Nick, look out!*"

Too late.

The critter uncoiled its body and leaped toward me in the dimness. I hit it with the only thing handy—my flashlight. It landed against its head with a solid 'thunk', and I foolishly expected the bastard to tumble down into the chasm below. But it somehow managed to use its near ten-foot long body to balance itself upon the edge of the shelf I stood upon long enough to reach over and sink its sharp talons into the chasm's wall.

Oh, shit!

Meanwhile, Ishi and Marie had lowered a rope to me. I mistakenly thought they might be attempting to rescue me from my unfortunate predicament. But then Ishi landed on the ledge behind me and away from the critter that was stealthily creeping toward me. Marie landed next to him.

Bad move on their parts. *Very* bad.

"What in the hell is that thing?" she whispered worriedly.

"I don't know—just something that's really hungry! Get your asses moving! *NOW!*"

Luckily, I noticed that the narrow ledge seemed a slight bit wider a short distance ahead of where Marie now ran. Apparently, she knew the path to potential safety was there, which brought my blood to a rapid boil. I shoved Ishi toward her, telling him to stay with her.

"What about you?!...And, what in the hell *is* that thing?"

I only saw his terrified look and his shaking hand for a moment while he pointed beyond me to the critter that had raised itself onto its hind legs.

"Just go, Ishi! I'll be along as soon as I take care of this asshole!"

I turned back to face our menace, hoping Ishi listened and got his ass in gear for his own good. I promised myself there would be a serious coming to Jesus moment between me and our debutante, whose sexiness was rapidly waning with me, once I made it out of this mess...if I made it out alive.

The critter hissed its displeasure. I suppose it wasn't accustomed to a potential meal fighting back. I had only a brief moment to consider what to do next. Should I turn around and run like the others? Or, should I stand my ground using a dented flashlight that now flickered on the verge of dying out? Tough decision and a bad time to be without a Ken Blanchard action plan.

Then I suddenly remembered the pickaxe strapped to my side. I couldn't believe I had forgotten it, swearing to the Good Lord that I would never drink my mind into such sluggishness the night before an expedition ever again.

Just let me kill this angry mother and...

It took a swipe at me, the wind lifting my bangs from my forehead as its claw just missed my face.

My turn.

Rather than spar with this thing, which I had little understanding of in the first place, I swung repeatedly with the axe, catching the tip in the critter's belly scales several times while it hissed angrily. One of the last blows came close to pay dirt, and I just knew the next shot would puncture its heart.

I prepared to slam the pickaxe into the critter's chest and brought my weapon down hard. But it had better reflexes than I had anticipated. It brought its left claw up to meet my right hand, and while I marveled at its sudden dexterity, the axe flew out of my hand and fell harmlessly into the chasm below.

Uh-oh.

Without a serviceable weapon, I was now officially screwed. Meanwhile, Marie and Ishi called for me from somewhere nearby…maybe fifty to seventy feet away. I turned toward their voices for just an instant, and the critter pounced.

It cost me my favorite hat. No, I didn't throw the damned thing at it—my cherished wide-brim fedora meant far too much for me to ever do something as drastic as that. However, sharp claws attempting to harpoon my skull and coming away with my preferred head cover instead certainly qualifies as a good reason not to mourn the loss.

At least it bought me time.

"Hurry, Nick! *Run!*"

"I'm coming!" I said, after turning around and running as fast as I could along the precarious pathway. "You two keep moving!"

"We *are!* Oh shit, it's coming after you—*watch out!*"

Marie was right…the bastard was pursuing me, crawling on its belly and snapping its menacing jaws at my feet. I felt the warmth of its breath upon my ankles. That spurred me on, and I sprinted blindly along the ledge, nearly falling into the abyss to my left more than once.

Despite Ishi and Marie's head start, I soon caught up to where they were, a mere twenty feet ahead of me, as we raced along the narrow path that seemed to take us even deeper into the earth. The humid smell of mold and decay surrounded us, and the sound of rushing water grew louder and louder in the darkness further below.

This was a bad place, where horrible events had happened. Intricately menacing glyphs covered the walls around us, revealed ever so briefly in the reflected glow of our flashlights.

But what in the hell good would it do any of us if we ended up as mid-afternoon snacks for the enraged critter keeping pace close behind? That thought became especially pertinent when the path ended abruptly.

And I mean abruptly.

One moment we were running, and the next the three of us were balancing on the edge of a sheer drop. Below, a surging, underground river poured from one dark opening and disappeared into another. More interesting was the fact that the water was glowing slightly green. I had seen this effect before. The green water was lit by the surrounding phosphorescent lichen.

Little good that did us, considering the thing chasing us had just appeared behind us.

"Oh, shit!" Marie murmured.

"Oh, shit, indeed," said I, casting an irritated glance at her before returning my gaze to the lizard-thing stealthily swaying back and forth. It prepared to launch itself at any of us.

Ishi looked wildly around himself and started speaking loudly in Tawankan. Sounded like gibberish even to me…but for some crazy reason, the critter suddenly backed off. It cocked its head as if mesmerized by Ishi's tribal mumbo-jumbo.

Hell, if it works, why knock it? Keep the pied-piper act going, little brother!

Meanwhile, we still had nowhere to go…or did we?

Marie aimed her flashlight at the wall and began smiling nervously, and then she giggled.

"What the hell's up with you?" I demanded. I had no doubt that Barney the Luminescent Dragon would come out of his spell at any moment. "I didn't sign up for this shit, and neither did Ishi!"

"I think I've got it," she said, looking relieved. "It makes sense when added to what I already knew about this place. I know what to do now."

"What in the hell are you talking about, now?"

This was getting weirder by the minute, and unfortunately Ishi's spell on the Minotaur that looked like a lizard was fading. The sucker eyed us dangerously again.

"We're not far from the first chamber...the door is somewhere close to us," she said, seemingly unaware of our renewed immediate danger. Her smile grew wider and her eyes almost sparkled with excitement. She looked damned sexy again. "Help me look for a small opening. A door, a lever...something! It's got to be around here some place..."

And there it was.

"Well, I be damned," I whispered, reverently looking down into the surging, foaming water. My apprehension melted into amazement.

And then, more appropriately, fear.

CHAPTER ELEVEN

"There," I said, pointing down.

Marie, who had been searching the face of the wall for the doorway, followed my pointing finger. "Where are you pointing to? The water?"

"Look, just below the surface, the dark opening."

She looked, leaning out over the ledge—started shaking her head. "Oh, no. No way."

She saw it as clearly as I did. The opening to another tunnel. Except this one was just below the foaming surface of the raging river. A shimmering black maw that awaited us.

"You can't be serious, Nick," she said, standing, suddenly pale.

"Hey, I didn't make the rules."

"*Compadre*," said Ishi, mixing his Tawankan with some Spanish. "You think you might want to give me a hand here?"

I stepped around Marie, who was only too happy to have a little more space between herself and whatever was still bearing down on Ishi.

Not that I didn't feel like we were moving in a blind panic. Still, a new vantage point allowed me a better assessment of the situation. And what I saw wasn't good—and it certainly wasn't natural.

Something new, and this thing creeping towards Ishi along the narrow ledge looked like a nightmare. No, it didn't look like one.

It was a nightmare.

It had human-enough looking legs and torso. After that, things got really bizarre. It's chest and arms were decidedly reptilian, and its head was for certain crocodilian. Or, as they're called in these parts, caimans. Speckled caimans, in fact. Central and South America's version of the crocodile. But it also resembled something else…something much more familiar.

What in the hell?

"Nick…" muttered Ishi, backing away—and into me.

As I mentioned, the beast was easily a foot or two taller than me, which would put the damned thing at least seven or eight feet tall. A lot of that height came from its extended, scaled neck.

Sweet Jesus.

Marie was suddenly behind me. Apparently, I had backed away, too, and into her. I knew we were all inches away from tumbling over the ledge. Still, the hulking half-man, half-caiman approached us. Its eyes were emerald slits of fire. Unnatural, and yet, could have been enhanced by the ambient phosphorescent light emanating from the river below.

Without realizing it, I had removed my Bowie knife. My cherished weapon that I had completely forgotten about! It felt good in my hand. It always felt good in my hand. I had used it to protect myself from wild boars, rabid dogs and one or two cutthroats in town. I've hunted with it and mastered it. It was my preferred weapon and tool of the trade, and as instinct took over, I was glad it was waiting and ready in my hand.

I touched Ishi's shoulder and my good friend jumped. But I needed my good friend out of the way, as I hate him fighting my fights.

He tore his frightened eyes off the approaching beast and looked at me. I had never known Ishi to be deeply scared—and especially not terrified to the core of his being. Then again, he and I had never faced such a walking nightmare.

I pointed to the knife and he got the idea. Without much room to maneuver in, he allowed me to step around him. Still, he stayed close behind me. Terrified or not, he wasn't going far. I heard him unbuckle his own knife and slide it free.

"What do you think it is?" he asked, whispering in my ear.

Marie heard him, and spoke behind us as I crouched lower, holding the knife out before me. The crocodile-man-thing paused only briefly, then picked up its speed as it approached.

"Ciudad Blanca is full of legend," said Marie, her words reaching me almost as an afterthought. I was completely focused on the creature coming at me. "The ancient ones living within these caves have been rumored to have perfected something close to bio-engineering long ago, along with their mastery of darker energies.... I think it's safe to say that these rumors were true."

"So this is the result of some ancient ritual gone bad?" I asked over my shoulder.

Her reply reached me distantly as the enraged critter sprinted toward us, its ghastly mouth fully open. "Those within Ciudad Blanca re-designed the human-genome to create hybrid human and animals."

Good information to know...especially yesterday, or even on the trip down inside this apparent death trap. But right then? Well, it was a little late. As she finished uttering those words, the monster suddenly launched itself into the air, its talons flayed out.

I'm fairly certain it didn't expect for me to leap as well. The beast and I crashed into each other in midair, and then landed hard on the slender ledge. There wasn't any way to prevent tumbling together into the frigid water of the underground river.

CHAPTER TWELVE

For a moment, I thought my final memory of this life would be of me drowning in the river's unknown depths. The creature had a distinct advantage—an amphibian advantage, that is. Since it could easily outlast me under water, I didn't have long before I'd either pass out from holding my breath, or endure the lizard-man's menacing bite. Which would be worse? Yeah, I honestly asked myself that question, and when I decided I'd prefer to die intact rather than bleeding from a fatal wound, I made one last desperate move.

I relaxed my grip on it's shoulders, hoping the damned thing would mistakenly think I had succumbed to its natural environment. I prayed like hell that it wasn't near as cunning as it seemed earlier. The monster reared back in preparation to bite my head off clean from my shoulders, and I pretended to be unconscious. For a moment, my hair drifted over my eyes in the water. But I was far more ready to launch into an attack than I let on. If the sucker really did have any human qualities, then I'm sure a serious moment of shock flew through it's brain as I deftly avoided its bite and then plunged the Bowie knife deep into its heart. If not for the soft, green glow surrounding us, I would've only felt the burst of warm blood spurting onto my arms in the cool depths of the river.

It can't be a normal reptile if the blood's warm... holy shit!

Its blood flowed quickly, and a cloud of deep crimson soon surrounded me. As the corpse drifted away, I caught a glimpse of something else moving rapidly towards me from further below. I would never survive another battle if I didn't get back to the surface first. I thrust myself upward, and must've briefly blacked out…. I heard someone calling to me from nearby.

Ishi?

I gasped for air, coughing as I tried to determine where the voice was coming from. Meanwhile, a large shadow passed between the dead lizard-man and me, and the ink-like cloud of blood dispersed as this new menace came within a few feet of my dangling legs.

Ishi called again…along with Marie.

"What? Where in the hell are you two?!"

Maybe I had died after all. When I scanned the ledge above me, I didn't see either one. But when their unified voices called to me again, I realized they were calling to me from inside the darkened hole in the earth that I had seen earlier. Their voices echoed eerily against the cave walls on either side of me.

"We're in *here!*" shouted Marie. "We're right in front of you, Nick!"

"No…no you can't be in there and talking—It's not frigging possible!"

I began to swim over to the river's edge, intending to try and scale the smooth walls that would get me back on top of the ledge.

"Look, you dumb ass—the river's running past us. You'll never make it out of here unless you join us, Nick!"

She sounded angry and at the same time pleading, which brought to mind images of Siren demons that were fabled to lead sailors to their graves on the high seas. Could this be a version of what Sirens are like a couple hundred feet below the earth's surface?

"She speaks the truth, Nick! I would not believe…but we stand here safe, watching the river flow by," said Ishi. "I told her to take her own damned chances, but she pulled me with her when she jumped into the hole. I'm sorry I didn't jump in to save you."

Not that either one could've saved me, since Ishi can't swim, and our Da Vinci girl doesn't look the alligator/crocodile wrestling type.

"Nick, you've got to trust us!" urged Marie. "Trust us before— oh shit, what is that thing behind you?!"

Well...let me see. It's bigger than the last critter, with longer, sharper teeth. No eyes—just glowing antennae, but with a mouth that looks as big as our four-wheeler waiting far above us...Hmm, I'd say it's just what we call a hungry mother that seems intent on taking a huge bite out of my ass, Marie!

"Okay, I'm coming!"

This latest aggressor skimmed toward me along the surface, half in and half out of the water. I suddenly pictured losing everything up to my Johnson if it re-submerged itself. That's all it took to get me moving again.

I breast-stroked it out of there quickly, wishing I'd given myself a better head start. I soon felt the thing's tentacles trying to grasp my pant legs. Were they barbed with painful poisonous tips? I sent a fervent prayer heavenward that the answer to that question would forever remain a mystery.

I heard Marie whimper, as if she might actually shed tears if I succumbed to my pursuer. "Nick, please quit screwing around!"

"Hurry up, man!" added Ishi.

"I'm coming! But, this had better not be a bunch of bullshit—Augh!"

As I approached the spot where I had heard their voices, I began to be sucked down into what looked like a whirlpool a few feet below the river's surface. As far as I could tell, my two options were either being eaten by the creature chasing my ass, or being sucked down into deeper depths. The water was much, much colder than where I had swam from. Of worse concern was the fact I couldn't see anything in the darkness ahead—not a damned thing. The luminescent creatures apparently liked the frigid water as much as I did.

The current suddenly pulled me under. This happened right after I cast an anxious glance over my shoulder at the big mother closing in from behind. It hovered close enough to where a sudden lunge would end my debate as to whether or not I'd find out if Ishi and Marie were still among the living.

Two pairs of hands grabbed my arms.

"Hold on Nick!"

The shrillness in Marie's voice sent an unpleasant ring through my right ear. In the next instant, I was lifted out of the water and then fell backward. Actually, it was more like being thrown into some sort of slimy foliage that resembled seaweed—at least the texture reminded me of the kelp beds I once played in when my dad briefly taught anthropology at UC Berkeley.

"Thank God you're okay!" She poked me in the darkness, and I realized she couldn't accurately determine where I was—despite the advantage she and Ishi had for their eyes to adjust to the darkness. "I really thought we'd lose you back there!"

So she really did weep, huh? At least a little bit.

"I'm fine, I think. That was close." True. But no broken bones, and my ass was still intact, despite the ache from when I had landed hard on the ledge during my battle with the lizard-man. "This is one jacked-up expedition you rooked us into, little lady. I think my retainer just doubled."

"Sounds good to me!" enthused Ishi.

"Always conniving, huh?" Marie sounded slightly amused, somewhat frightened, and a whole lot of annoyed. "Sure, I could pay you that…but it would reduce your take on the treasure, once we find it."

I couldn't see her clearly enough yet, but pictured her smirk. I detected the outline of someone standing where I heard her feet kick away rocks and the weird kelp-like shit lying in abundance around our feet.

"I don't suppose your map is going to help us anytime soon. Do either of you still have a flashlight?"

"Mine fell into the river," said Ishi. "I was trying to catch your leg when you slid off the ledge. It fell out of my hand."

"How about you, Princess D?"

Marie's silence told me she was in no mood to kid around. Yes, things were looking grim, but I've always found that in the bleakest moments laughter inspires ingenuity.

"Mine quit working shortly after we left the other level."

"You shouldn't have bought them at K-Mart."

"There isn't a K-Mart here in Honduras, smart ass!"

"What's K-Mart?" Ishi sounded confused.

"What they don't have in Honduras," I said. "Apparently, finding a good flashlight in these parts is like finding a woman with an agreeable temperament."

"I suppose that's supposed to be funny?" Marie sounded even less amused.

"Yep…just not in—"

"Don't say it, Nick!" Her voice was closer, as if she had just walked back toward me. "I'm starting to freak out a little…this is supposed to be where my father found the secret passage. But without a light we'll never find it. *Shit!*"

She fished out her cell phone from her front pocket. It was one of those smart phone deals that had lots of gadgets, none of which were protection from water.

"It's ruined!" she lamented.

I should've anticipated this happening at some point. Marie hadn't come across as a female prone to panic. But, the rising tension in her tone told me it was coming soon.

"Are you expecting a call?" I asked.

"Don't be such a jerk, Nick. My phone had everything. GPS, maps, satellites…hell, even a light."

"I'm sorry for your loss."

"It's *our* loss. Shit, shit, *shit!*"

"You're right," I said. "What will we do now without an iPhone to guide our way?"

"You're working my last nerve, Nick Caine."

I chuckled and so did Ishi. Neither of us used such phones or gadgets. Sure, I had an old cell that worked half the time.

Other than that, we used maps, compasses, flashlights, and even firelight, if need be. I said as much to her.

"I like my phone," she said. "It's better than your old-fashioned way of doing business. I feel safe with my phone."

"It sounds like you and your phone might need some time apart."

Something loud and sharp filled the small cavern. The noise, amazingly came from Marie's throat…and her frustrated scream was soon followed by something else.

"What in the hell's up with you now?"

Now, she was working my last nerve.

"I'm…I'm…hype…hyperventilating."

"Because you ruined your iPhone?"

"Yuh..yes."

I rolled my eyes, despite the fact that no one could see me. "Jesus. Well, try to relax, will you? You're not helping anything."

I left Miss Da Vinci to figure out how she would live life without her iPhone and found Ishi in the dark. Not too hard to do since he was chuckling lightly.

"Your girlfriend is funny," said Ishi.

"She's not my girlfriend," I said irritably.

He chuckled some more, then grew somber. After a moment, he asked, "So, how'd they travel through here in the old days?"

"Hey, you're right," I said, surprised I hadn't asked myself this question yet. "There's got to be a torch somewhere along the walls. Marie, check the cave wall to our left, and I'll check the one to our right. If it follows what we've seen in other older caves in this part of the world, we shouldn't have to search for long."

"I'll look for two rocks to create a spark," said Ishi. "We can use our clothes and my pickaxe handle to make a torch."

"Great thinking, as long as something's dry…you won't find a dry stitch on me," I said. "Let's see what we can come up with in here…just try not to get bit by anything."

"By what?" asked Marie, worriedly.

"Spiders, bats, snakes, things like that," said Ishi, his tone nonchalant.

I could almost hear her gingerly touching the walls....

"Maybe I should handle this on my own," I suggested. "You can't treat this like a country club luncheon, Marie. Just work your hands through the webs and whatever else is stuck to the walls, and—"

"Got it!" she cried out.

"So you know what I'm getting at?"

"No, I mean I am holding a torch!" she advised, and I could hear the triumph in her voice. "Give me your lighter."

"My what...oh, shit. Here it is," I said, after fishing it out. Yeah, I know. I should've thought of it right away. But I thought I'd left it with my smokes in the Jeep. "It might not work after taking a bath in the river."

But it did work, and I saw that she was indeed holding a torch. Not an ancient one, which was probably a good thing, although it wasn't exactly a recent torch either. "You're father's old torch?"

"Undoubtedly!" she said, triumphantly.

"Why would he leave his torch behind?" I wondered aloud

"Hard to say," she said, immediately bringing the torch up closer to the wall closest to her, where several rows of pictograms had been carved into it. "There could have been a number of such torches. Perhaps they left this one behind for the way back."

I nodded. Leaving a marker behind—a torch, in this case—was a good idea, actually.

Ishi's primitive skills might've come in handy, but he was just as happy to deposit the two small flint-like pieces he had recovered from the cave floor into his pants pocket.

"I told you I thought this was the right place where we needed to be. The signs are right here!" Marie enthused, as she held up the torch to another wall covered with primitive writing that I didn't recognize. Even relic hunters know their way around Mayan and pre-Mayan glyphs, but we can be stumped. "I realize that none of us can read what has been inscribed here, but the map has a key. I've memorized most of it, so let's see if I can figure this out without having to dig it out of my...oh shit, where did I set my fanny pack?"

"Ishi, check her fanny," I said, unable to resist one more zinger.

Ishi chuckled and said, "She took it off on the ledge when we were all being chased."

"Great, just lovely," she murmured, then grew silent as she studied the wall. Ishi and I watched as she silently mouthed her pronunciation of the symbols, reading from a line that ran across the middle of this particular wall. A moment later, she started to grin...and then her grin soon morphed into a look of childlike fascination. "It's here...somewhere in this room!"

"What's in the room?" I asked, while Ishi and I followed Marie as her frantic gaze moved from wall to wall.

"The doorway to the tunnel that leads directly to the treasures we seek is in one of these walls," she said, moving quickly, stepping over scattered stones. "What the glyphs just now revealed is the corresponding symbol that won't be as easy to...Ishi, would you mind holding the torch for a moment? This might be what we're looking for."

Ishi held the torch as high as he could and Marie dusted aside a spider's web and its makers, now totally unconcerned about a potential bite. Funny what getting close to a treasure does to someone. She was standing before the flattest section of the wall, alternately wiping and blowing away dust.

She pointed excitedly. "Oh, my God...it sure looks like what Dad described to me six years ago, and it fits what was described in the map." She indicated more glyphs that I didn't recognize. At least not at first. These glyphs were identical to the ones on the other wall. Corresponding glyphs, perhaps.

Most importantly, just below the glyphs, which I understood now were markers, she pointed to something small and protruding from the wall. A stone lever. It made me a tad uneasy as she reached for it. "I hope this is what I believe it is."

"Me, too, sister," I said, as she pulled on the lever.

Immediately, the ground began to shake. Ishi grabbed onto Marie, who grabbed onto me. Not quite the threesome I had in mind. A moment later the wall opened up. From beyond the wall, a golden haze greeted us.

"What in the hell?"

CHAPTER THIRTEEN

"I thought you said this was where the treasure was," I said.
"No," said Marie, stepping forward and shielding her eyes,
"I said this was the tunnel that led to the treasure."

"And where would the treasure be?" I asked.

"That," she said, turning to me and smiling as golden sunlight
washed over her alabaster skin, "is the million dollar question."

"How about a ten million dollar question, instead?" I said.

Beyond, birds twittered. A howler monkey shrieked.
Something heavy moved through the thick underbrush near the
tunnel's exit, then abruptly dashed off. Marie glanced briefly
through the doorway, then back at me. "If the legends are even
a fraction true, we might be looking at billions."

"You never said anything about billions," I said. Ishi had
stepped up behind me...and promptly dashed out the torch, its
flame now unnecessary.

"Perhaps many billions, Mr. Caine."

"That's if Ciudad Blanca exists," I said.

"For a treasure hunter, Mr. Caine, you're surprisingly cynical."

"Yeah, well, I've been burned one too many times. And I
smell smoke all over this."

She reached back and gently patted my face, a simple ges-
ture that sent a thrill through me. Dammit. "Well, my doubting
Thomas, there's only one way to find out."

And I really shouldn't have been very surprised when she
pushed aside a tangle of spider webs and marched through the

narrow tunnel, her shapely figure now silhouetted against the bright light.

"The girl has guts," said Ishi.

"I know," I said, stepping forward, "It's beginning to annoy me."

———

The tunnel opened up into what appeared to be a deep valley. To either side rose steep cliffs covered in dense foliage. Before us was a rock-strewn path through even denser undergrowth. What lay beyond was anyone's guess.

We caught up to Marie. Or, more accurately, she waited for us. Impatiently. Literally tapping her foot and folding her arms. Yeah, she was all types of bugging me.

We continued along with Ishi now in the lead. The Tawankan was unusually skilled at wielding his machete, which he did now, hacking a path for us through the vine-covered trail.

The jungle seemed particularly alive. Trees shook with the passage of various monkey species: howler, spider, squirrel monkeys, capuchins, tamarins…and a species I didn't readily recognize. A larger species with long, shaggy hair. It swung easily in the branches above, moving with cat-like grace and agility, and watching us closely.

Ishi saw it, too, and paused briefly, machete raised high. I could be wrong, but I might have seen the Tawankan shiver slightly. Never a good sign. After a moment, he continued hacking and we continued following.

We did this for some time, following a hint of a game trail that meandered deeper into the valley. What valley? I hadn't a clue. I thought I knew Honduras. In fact, I thought I knew it like the proverbial back of my hand. The same hand that sported a half dozens circular scars that were, unsurprisingly, the exact circumference of a piranha's mouth. Long story.

We paused for some water a few hours in, finding a moss-covered log that could seat three and was critter free. It was coming on early evening and the sun had slipped behind the western valley wall. Soon, we were going to be in complete darkness. Not anything I hadn't experienced hundreds of times before. Hell, half my life had been spent camping in the wilds. But, something about this valley was…unnerving.

"Where are we?" asked Marie.

She had already capped her water bottle, and I could tell she was picturing the contours of the map she had lost. Even so, she still held her iPad. Holding it like she was hoping against hope that the GPS finder would suddenly spring to life. Ishi glanced at the iPad briefly, wrinkled his nose and turned away while stifling a snicker. He studied the trees above us, which was never a bad idea when one was in the deep, dark jungle.

Despite the fact I was now seriously concerned that we would soon be lost without a clue as to where to go next, I followed Marie's muttered words and her pointing finger as she backtracked our progress along the dirt road we had followed in the jeep, and the path we had hiked along to reach the tunnel. She then pointed to the tunnel's exit we had recently emerged from. She frowned.

We had ended up deep within the mountains, and then had made a mad dash for our lives when the lizard man had appeared. Where we had now ultimately ended up was beyond even my own inner compass.

I told her as much, in which she responded, "You just might be the first man to admit he doesn't know where he is."

Thus far, Marie tended to lash out when she didn't get what she wanted, or heard what she wanted. But, for the moment she remained calm…at least externally. I was almost content to let sleeping dogs lie.

"Ishi, do you know where we are?"

"No clue, Nick," he said, still scanning the trees. Something was triggering his inner alarm system. Ishi was like my watchdog. The Tawankan seemed to have a sixth sense for spotting trouble.

"There you go," I said to Marie. "Two men who admit to not knowing where they are."

And then I saw it. Fifty feet away something was slowly, carefully parting the branches of a wax palm. Ishi, I was certain, had seen it, too, but he made a point to look away. Good idea. I looked away, as well, although I kept the slightly moving branches in my periphery.

Marie snickered tiredly and turned away.

"I can tell you this: we're in a valley of sorts," I said. "It doesn't look like one of the hotter tourist stops Honduras has to offer, does it?"

"Thank you, Magellan."

I chuckled, all the while keeping my main focus on the shadow that was still present behind the parted branches of the dense wax palm.

"Well, there's one thing I find interesting," I continued. "It's a misleading valley, you see. It's far wider at the base than at the apex."

"What do you mean?"

"We're given the false impression that we're in some forest, or a part of the forest."

"We're not in a forest?" She sounded alarmed, as if she suddenly didn't know where she was.

"No," I said, reaching inside my still-wet jacket and withdrawing the Bowie knife, a knife that had, amazingly, found its way back into its sheath. My Bowie and me…it's a beautiful thing.

"Then what do you call this?" she asked, standing and motioning at the dense foliage around us.

"A lost valley," I said. "Now get down."

"What?"

"Get down!"

CHAPTER FOURTEEN

No sooner had we fallen prostrate upon the ground than something enormous flew past our heads. It was an animal with black fur, and as it tumbled into a banana palm behind us, it let out an angry growl.

Oh sweet Jesus, what in the hell was that?!

"What in the hell was that?" whimpered Marie, echoing my alarmed silent thought.

"I don't know exactly," I told her, squinting my eyes in the ever-growing dimness.

"Exactly? So that should mean you know something of what it is…right?"

Even in times of duress, she still had to be an academic smart ass. Something in common between us, which made her even more attractive. At the same time, it also upped the ante on how irritating she could be.

"Well, no. Exactly could mean nothing more than 'it ain't exactly Smokey the Bear'," I said, glancing back at the beast that regarded us warily as it regained its footing. It would be back for round two at any moment. "In fact, I don't think it's a bear at all."

"It looks like a big dog or a cat," said Ishi, nervously. "It's too big to be a jaguarundi"

"A *what?*" said Marie, inching closer to me, to where her light perfume filled my nostrils. "All I know is that thing's huge!"

True. It certainly wasn't the cougar-sized jaguarundi. The monster was far too big. But once it focused its luminescent yellow eyes upon us, I could tell it was the bigger cousin of the aforementioned jaguarundi. A panther. Black as midnight with a blue sheen running through its fur. And, bigger than any other panther I'd ever come across.

"Well…what in the hell *is* it?"

The shrillness was back in Marie's voice.

"You should know, since it's the creature depicted on your papa's treasured disk," I said, finding it impossible to not snicker. It's a nervous tic of mine. "And before you try to tell me this ain't a jaguar, think again—"

"Yeah, I know, Nick—they're part of the panthera family of big cats," she said, interrupting me. Her tone sounded even more worried. "But I never expected to encounter anything quite that big. Papa said to watch out for the jaguars that guard the entrance to the 'treasure cave'."

"*What?!* So, you knew about this damned thing and never said a word about it? And, there's more than this one??"

"Yes. But, if we move quickly, we should be able to get inside before anything bad happens."

"Bad? What do you mean by 'bad'??"

Ishi's voice cracked as he said this. Meanwhile, the enormous panther began to creep toward us. Its yellow eyes were tinged with orange halos around the edges, as if the very fires of hell had ignited them. No, I didn't think that thought right away…it was what popped in my head for a brief moment as I turned to follow Marie as she sprinted toward a group of gnarled trees near where our jaguar friend had originally been peering at us.

"*Where in the hell are you running to?*" I called after her, after urging Ishi to quit staring stupidly at the big cat and hightail his ass to join mine in pursuit of our more athletic female companion. "*Shit!*…Ishi, damn it let's go!!"

"I'm coming, Nick! I'm—ah, shit, it's coming after us!!"

As if the jaguar's menacing growl hadn't already announced that fact. As much as I worried that we were chasing a mad woman into our death trap, the reality that an animal large enough to devour my diminutive companion in a couple of bites and me in under five provided all the incentive needed to for us to sprint into the shadowed foliage ahead of us.

"Nick—get ready to dive!"

"Huh?! Are you frigging serious? Dive *where??*"

"Both of you need to dive headfirst when I tell you to do it!" Marie shouted back toward me. I couldn't see her, and I started to slow down so I could get my bearings. It seemed like the smartest thing to do.

"No! Nick, keep running! You're almost there! I remember it…everything's coming back to me. Get ready to—*oh shit!"*

"Marie?! What in the…. Are you all right—"

"Dive, damn it—*do it now!"*

But there was no response. Nothing. Well, check that…I heard several low growls in the deep shadows within the shade from the native palms, shrubs, and other broad-leaved plants. It sounded like there were a dozen big cats, although I only caught a glimpse of another pair of luminous eyes—this time orange. It seemed odd that the jaguar had companions, since they are solitary critters. But, when the eyes disappeared from view, none of that mattered. I knew instinctively that this particular cat was circling around us and that an attack might well ensue at any moment.

We were in a terrible spot. Yeah, no kidding…I wanted to warn Ishi, but as I turned to look back at him, my feet gave out from under me and I landed hard on my ass once more. This time it felt like a stone slide.

Oh, shit!!

I would like to tell you that it was a heavy-masculine thing that came out of my mouth in this latest moment of surprise. However, I must confess that a shrill scream that would rival any little girl's frightened shriek escaped my throat instead. It didn't matter that Marie had tried to warn me about what lay ahead. Not that plunging another few hundred feet or so down a cold, grime-covered chute surrounded by pitch-blackness wouldn't prompt most males to utter a terrified response of some sort. That would have been my second excuse. The initial one? My rationale that I was actually frightened for Ishi. Hell, he might not have heard Marie's warning either, and would soon become what amounted to a Happy Meal for the apparent protectors of this chasm.

I heard a surprised yelp from Marie up ahead, which told me that I deserved partial credit for descending down the correct rabbit hole. A small pinpoint of light soon greeted my eyes up ahead, as my body picked up speed. I would reach this mysterious glow that rapidly grew bigger in the next ten to fifteen seconds. Meanwhile, Ishi's piercing shriek resounded behind me, which made me feel a little better about my reaction. Although, I initially feared he had failed to elude the enormous panther, or one of its companions. I would never want him to see me shed a tear—either in this life or the next—but I felt choked up, thinking of his unpleasant fate and ignoring the fact that Marie's and mine might well be worse.

"Nick?"

It sounded like an echo...Marie's voice? Likely, and she called to me from just beyond the light that was now a few feet in diameter. The light suddenly flickered upon my approach, and I realized it was caused by another torch. My journey was about to end, and I would reach my destination in a moment.

"Holy mother of Jesus!!!"

I flew out of the chute and grazed the back of my head as I emerged airborne.

"Be careful, Nick!"

Now she tells me. I landed hard yet again...at least this time I landed on my back instead of my ass. But a rear-end landing would've been better, as I landed hard enough to where the blow knocked the wind out of me. Marie's panicked voice soon followed, along with another, closer, shriek from Ishi. Their voices grew faint as my awareness of the world around me began to fade.

My little feisty companion lives to fight another day! Excellent news! But Marie sounds like she's already started bitching at me about something again...my God...this place is glowing! There's gold everywhere...

It was my last thought before blacking out.

CHAPTER FIFTEEN

I t's hard to say how long I was out.

When I regained consciousness, Marie and Ishi were standing over me. Check that…they were kneeling over me, their faces drawn close to mine as their blurred images soon became clearer.

"Well, it's about time," said Marie, her tone and smile playful. She was in a damned good mood about something…and it surely had to do with the golden glow around me. "We've got just enough water to last until afternoon," she added, "but I think you should take a few sips."

She held out the canteen that had been strapped to her waist. The water tasted and felt good…but I only took a couple of sips before sitting up to look around me.

"Holy…"

I couldn't finish voicing the thought in my head. By then, Marie had lit three other torches in the immense room that was stacked high with golden trinkets, vessels, statues, and what looked like octagonal coins. All of it gleamed in haphazard array, and most was covered by cobwebs from centuries past, along with layers of dust and grime. But it all simply added to the wonder and magic of this moment.

I tried again. "This really does look like it could be worth a billion or two."

"Or three," said Maria. "According to my father, who cataloged what is here long ago, the gold would've been worth well over a billion dollars five to ten years ago." She flashed the same smile of amazement that I could feel stretching across my face. "Even if we can only remove a small portion of this, none of us will have to worry about money ever again."

"Well...other than scooping up enough items to fill our pockets, it does seem like we will have to take a few trips going back and forth to the Jeep," I said, trying to not sound cynical since she willingly shared what was nearly the end of her personal water supply. Ishi and I already had to fend for ourselves after draining our disposable bottles of water right before our unforeseen tussle with the lizard-man.

"No, we won't!" said Ishi triumphantly, holding up several large bags. Clearly he'd checked the place out while I was busy being useless. "Marie's father left these. Here, take one."

He held out a bag that appeared to be army-issued, although the original green dye had greatly faded in the material. Then again, maybe it wasn't army-issued to begin with. But the bag was definitely a strong heavy-duty grade—suitable for miners and legit archaeologists. Therefore, it was good enough for me.

"As much as I'd like to bask in the gilded light of Xanadu," I said, standing on legs that felt weak at best, "we need to grab what we can and then secure the place. It might be a while before we make it back here."

I couldn't imagine coming back via the way we came here the first time, and since we couldn't go back that way either, we would have to find a different—and likely longer—way out of this valley. Of course, that was after we figured out how to escape this vault that had to be located several hundred feet below the earth's surface.

No sooner than I thought these thoughts, Marie said, "After we gather what we can comfortably carry, father mentioned another exit from the room, an exit that will take us into a cave system that is not so hard to navigate."

Both Ishi and I turned toward her with near-matching looks of surprise.

"You've got to be friggin' kidding me!" I seethed, feeling the headache that was starting to wane suddenly grow more intense again. "Are you saying we didn't have to go the route we took—that there was an easier way to get down here?"

"Yes," she replied meekly. "But the easier path is known to my Uncle Leo—at least partially so. I saw one of his henchmen near my hotel this morning before I came to get you. It was too risky to go that route, since I knew you could get us through safely if I chose to take the more dangerous caverns instead."

"Wait…wait a moment," I said, shaking my head. "So, you see one of the killers that works for Uncle Leo just hanging around the Sheraton you're staying at, and you don't think that maybe he and your uncle have at least a pretty good idea of the location you are going to, huh? Is that what you're telling me?!"

"Yes," she again replied, this time even more demurely. "But, we couldn't wait around to see what my uncle was up to. After all, he's never been here before, since he is missing several access key landmarks that are difficult to discern on his map—landmarks that I've memorized."

"Well, sweetheart, that's all fine and dandy…except for the fact I noticed a gray sedan following us out of the city limits," I said, feeling a growing knot of dread in my gut.

Damn it! I *knew* something was up and didn't say a frigging thing!

"I saw it, too," she confessed. "But it wasn't the only gray Mercedes on the road."

I looked over at Ishi, who was shaking his head…either at Ms. Da Vinci's and my latest squabble, or the fact we were standing around while he loaded his bag. He might look like a small fry, but I've seen him hoist a two hundred-pound backpack before. He might well carry double what our princess-in-waiting and me picked up.

Mindful of the fact that it was now a very bad idea to linger in this amazing place, I scanned the room for possible intruders and possible exits alike.

"Well, I think assuming anything about a ruthless, greedy son-of-a-bitch is foolish. Leo the asshole could show up sometime soon...."

Suddenly, a few small rocks tumbled down upon one of the bigger piles of gold that stretched upward to just below the cave room's stalactite-covered ceiling. Next to it appeared to be an exit that had looked the most promising in my earlier survey. Except now three men stood in front of it, and two were armed with automatic weapons. The other man was someone I recognized from a bad experience a few years earlier.

"So, I see that we meet again, Nick Caine," the man said coldly, mimicking a line spoken in dozens, if not hundreds of movies. "How lovely."

He looked both amused and pissed. But that wasn't the biggest thing I noticed about this man. Time can often be unkind to human beings. In this case, it had been extremely cruel to Leonardo Da Vinci.

CHAPTER SIXTEEN

"What in the hell are you doing here?" Marie demanded. "Why, my dear girl…is that any way to address your dear uncle?"

"Eat shit and die, asshole!"

Ishi and I looked at each other warily. We had seen the good, the bad, and the incredibly mysterious aspects that marked Marie's personality. Too late to wish she had pulled a far more diplomatic card to play here, it didn't take a rocket scientist's analysis to know we were totally screwed. And barring a miraculous escape presenting itself, we might soon become a trio of rotting corpses replacing the vast fortune of gold in this cavern.

"Oh, come now, Marie…you are embarrassing yourself in front of your new pals," he said, his tone only slightly less acerbic. "Not to mention that you've hurt my feelings."

"Feelings? How dare you talk of human qualities, you conniving snake!" she hissed in fury. "Why, if I can find a way, I'll—"

That's when I reached over and brought her close to me, effectively making it look like there might be something between us, while finding a way to slow down the death wish pouring out of her gorgeous mouth. Of course, she slammed her elbow into my side, letting me know in no uncertain terms that she was less than enamored with my forced intimacy—especially right then.

"Oh, how touching," said Leo, wearing a contemptuous smirk. "Perhaps if some foolish tourist is curious enough to venture down into the caverns that lead to this soon-to-be depleted room filled with my gold, they will marvel at your intertwined carcasses. By then, the two of you will be picked clean by insects and all sorts of slithering creatures pleased to have their home back after centuries in exile…"

He went on talking, but by then I had already tuned out the monotonous drone of his nasally voice. As I mentioned, time had been unkind to Marie's uncle, whose dull brown eyes spoke to the man's soullessness. Frankly, I was surprised that he had bothered with the journey down into the earth, instead of leaving everything up to his henchmen. The considerable girth on his six-four frame seemed to have doubled since the last time we crossed paths—an encounter that nearly spelled the end of my earthly stay. Yet another story for later.

But the point of this is that I was actively looking for an angle to play. Otherwise, his threats to end his niece's and my existence would surely come to pass…and soon.

"So, I take it we can't arm wrestle for a winner-take-all resolution, huh?" I said as soon as he finished his eloquent dribble.

And, yeah, Marie flinched while Ishi looked over at me as if I'd completely lost my frigging mind. But I was banking on the fact Leo's henchmen's semi-automatic rifles were trained in general on us and not upon our heads just yet. The mercenary look of these guys made it obvious that when it was time to bid us *adios*, the weapons would be raised and our foreheads would be their close range targets. That meant I had about twenty seconds still to come up with an escape plan.

"Always the joker, Nicholas," he laughed, although the glint of amusement in his eyes had disappeared. "I've often wondered if we should've fed you to the Nile crocs and not your buddy, Mario, ten years ago. Or…perhaps we should have fed you both, and then called it a day."

"Maybe," I said, noticing that the biggest 'hill' that was made of thousands of golden trinkets, figurines, and small bowls had a narrow stalactite above it. The distance was within my throwing range. Could I hit it? Perhaps…as long as I had the right item to toss. A better question would be whether or not it would make a difference, since the stalactite's tip would have to crack off and land upon the hill's apex perfectly to cause the avalanche I hoped for. "Mario was a good man, and a better friend. And I have no doubt that he's waiting on your sorry ass to join him for an ass-kicking the very moment you cross over into the afterlife."

Words delivered smoothly, and it got the reaction I wanted... the one I desperately needed to try and work my even more desperate plan. Leo gave in to an uproarious fit of laughter, and even his two assassins began chuckling. These guys looked eastern-European, and I worried the joke might be lost on them. But the laughter grew as Leo's fit continued. This was it—the now-or-never moment I needed.

I pulled Marie close and planted the most intense kiss upon her mouth. Of course, she squealed in surprise and tried to push me away. But she held on long enough for me to reach between us and grab my beloved bowie knife. The very bowie knife that my dad once wore on his utility belt, and the one that *always* felt good in my hand.

No, I didn't try to use it on our assailants. That would've been suicide.

But, I did use it.

Knowing I'd likely never see it again if my plan failed or was successful, I flung it by the sharp tip toward the stalactite high above us. It twirled in the air, and flew with the familiar 'swoosh' from whenever I'd thrown the damned thing with force in the past. The knife hit the point exactly where I had hoped...and then careened off and clanked loudly against the cavern wall to our right.

The stalactite remained intact.

Ishi let out a low sigh that was followed by a low grown, and then Marie began to berate me about my kiss. The menacing trio standing in front of us no longer found my behavior amusing, and as the gunmen repositioned their weapons I couldn't help but smile at the irony of my last moments on earth. Why in the hell had I thought hitting a bull's eye on a target sixty feet away would amount to more than a pile of bat dung in the end?

But the expected gunfire—either as single shots or a barrage of bullets—didn't happen. It didn't because in that moment of expecting to die, while everything grew eerily quiet around me, I was largely unaware of a loud rumble going on in the wall where my knife had struck.

"Oh, my God, Nick—you hit the jaguar's eye!" said Marie, excitedly.

"The what?!"

But then I saw what she was talking about, and felt somewhat ashamed that I had paid little attention to the carvings upon that wall. Especially the one that marked this cavern as the inner sanctuary of what long ago was known by the moniker *"Templo Del Jaguar"*, as Cortez once referred to this mystical place. My knife had chipped a small portion of the eye, which apparently set off a trigger of some sort. The wall was moving backward, and as it did the other walls and the floor below us began to shake.

"It's collapsing!" shouted Ishi, no longer worried about the scary men holding assault rifles. "We've got to go!"

"You're not going anywhere!" sneered Leo, who had removed a pistol from his belt. It looked like a Beretta, but too much was shaking for me to say for certain. He pointed the gun at us, when it seemed to me it would be easier to have his hired hands do the intimidation or shooting for him. "Since it looks like I'll have to come back, we'll kill you three now and worry about the mess later. We'll—"

The hill of gold suddenly collapsed, and it did so much more magnificently than I had pictured in my head. Untold tons of glittering yellow metal landed on all three of the bastards. Leo screamed in pain after being knocked to the ground, his legs completely submerged. Blood seeped from his visible lower extremities, while he writhed in terrible agony. Meanwhile, the other two men had disappeared...buried completely.

But the violent surge through the floor and walls continued unabated.

"Do you know the way out of here!" I shouted above the din toward Marie, who was scanning the surrounding walls in panic.

"I think it's this way," she said, pointing behind us.

"Huh?! What about where your uncle and his cronies emerged from, up there?"

I pointed to the cavern entrance that was perhaps thirty feet above us, after first stepping on Leo's hand and then confiscating his prized Cold War weapon. Hell, despite his immediate hardship, it seemed like I deserved something in trade for my knife.

"Oh, yeah," said Marie. "That might be better!"

In other words, Marie had no clue.

It was up to me, since Ishi had gone nuts and was acting like the dumb asses in those famous mummy movies from a few years back, filling his canvas bag with as much gold as he could carry. Hopefully, he wouldn't meet a similar demise to what Hollywood usually delivered for such foolish avarice.

"All right everyone, let's go! Come on, Ishi! We've got to get out of here *now!!*"

By then the walls and ceiling were crumbling with dangerous chunks of rock falling toward us. Even the other golden mounds of untold value were disintegrating. I looked down in time to see a three-foot fissure form in the floor. This place was going down, and very soon. To Hell? Quite possibly...or at least to a place with lava running through it. That's how it looked to me, for inside the fissure I saw a brilliant orange glow far below.

"Come on, you two—get a frigging move on it!!"

We clambered onto the narrow walkway that would lead to the small cavern mouth above. I think we all knew instinctively that we had about a minute to escape this particular cavern. Surprisingly, Ishi kept up, despite the pay-dirt load he carried over his shoulder. As soon as we reached the cavern mouth, the floor below gave way, as if whatever force had kept it together had done so for our benefit only. The river of lava below engulfed the horde of gold, along with the shrieking evil uncle of Marie Da Vinci.

I'd never seen anything like this in the thirty-four years I've been riding mother earth. But, I damned well knew that hanging around in a now-volatile cave system was a bad idea. A very bad idea, as it turned out.

I pushed Marie and Ishi in front of me as we climbed through a narrow tunnel that felt like it stretched for miles, and brought incredible discomfort to my legs as we kept a strenuous pace toward the surface. All of us faced pitch-blackness ahead, clinging to the slim hope that we wouldn't fall into a deep chasm we couldn't detect in advance.

Finally, another tiny pinpoint of light appeared, and Marie was the first to announce it as she raced toward it. By then, Ishi was exhausted from the heavy load he carried. So, being the gentleman I rarely am, I lifted the load from his back and sent him on to catch up to our suddenly re-energized femme fatale.

It almost proved to be my undoing.

As I pursued them, finding it nearly impossible to maintain a quick pace, the collapse from far below suddenly expanded to include the tunnel I desperately sought to escape. I heard the explosion first, and knew that whatever volatile forces had created the initial collapse were now spreading rapidly toward the cave system's perimeter.

"Hurry, Nick!" Marie shouted back to me.

I looked up toward the place where she and Ishi waited, just outside the tunnel's entrance, as stinging sweat poured into my eyes. The stars and the light from a late night moon illuminated the sky behind them.

"I'm try-trying," I gasped, and then decided to save my breath, and instead concentrate on reaching the exit.

I almost made it to where they waited before the final collapse hit, as the ancient volcano sought to reclaim much of the lava cone it had first created many eons ago. As it was, I at least had the good sense to thrust Ishi's bag of goodies out through the tunnel's mouth before the floor below me finally gave way.

"Oh, shit!"

"Nick, hang on!"

As the floor disappeared into a soup of earth and molten rock several hundred feet below me, I grabbed onto the root of a large tree growing just outside the tunnel. I didn't know if I could hang on long enough or if the root would hold without breaking off. Much too quickly, my tired hands started to slide down.

If it had been just one of my companions fighting to save me, I doubt I'd be telling this story now. But the combination of Ishi and Marie's desperate pulls on my arms and shirt proved enough to lift me out of the hole.

The fresh air alone was enough to revive my senses, although it was laced with the same rotten sulfuric stench we had dealt with for the past couple of hours. When I was able to stand again, the view before me seemed even more surreal than what we'd already experienced. Below us sat the expanding maw of a churning lake of fire that was already several acres wide. It seemed to be receding back into the earth. I watched as rocks, trees and other debris were quickly absorbed. A spectacular and deadly sight, it stirred something inside me. Especially when I looked over at the two beautiful faces that regarded me with soiled but serene expressions.

Gratitude. I felt grateful for life, true friendship, and the possibility of love. I was truly thankful to still be alive.

CHAPTER SEVENTEEN

"How much can you give me for the both of them?"
Juan Esteban eyed me curiously as I asked the question. Rather than answer right away, he held the intricately carved gold earrings up to his jeweler's glass once more.

"Do you want the money today?"

"Yes."

"And, will you take a check?"

"No, *hombre*," I said, chuckling. "Just like always, it's cash-ola only. Preferably in American dollars."

"You sound like a man who is desperate to leave Honduras... no?"

Now Juan chuckled.

"I might be back in a few months," I said. "And, if and when I do, you'll be the first artifacts dealer I visit."

"Careful, Nick...you make me feel not so clean when you describe me like that." He chuckled again, turning in his chair as he reached for a bigger magnifier to work with. "I'll give you twenty thousand dollars today...in your American cash. That's a fair price."

"Really?" I snickered, and I could tell as he looked up sharply from his viewer that he expected another Nick-barb was on its way. "Nah, I'm not here to give you hell, man. You've done well by me over the years. But the least you could do is offer me half of the eighty Gs street value these items have."

"I did offer you half…it's twenty thousand a piece," he said, smiling I'm sure in response to the subtle look of surprise written upon my face. "You're about to walk out of here with forty Gs, my friend. Forty Gs is enough to get lost for six months."

"Or longer, if one knows how to spend it right…and where to spend it."

"So, we have a deal?" he asked.

"Absolutely."

He reached over the counter and we shook hands. It was the longest handshake that Juan and I had ever shared in the six years I had known him. The mistiness in his eyes confirmed that he thought the same thing as me. This would likely be the last time we would ever do business like this, and even more likely, we would never see each other again.

"How did it go?" asked Marie, once I locked my seatbelt in the passenger seat of her rented Jeep.

Ishi sat in the back seat, sporting the new outfit he had splurged on at a local clothing shop. Of course, Marie was as beautiful as ever, dressed in a low cut blouse and slim fitting jeans, along with…. Oh sweet Jesus, why do women wear high heels with jeans? Yeah, she looked amazing, but I'm a practical sort of guy who has a hard time wrapping my mind around the style-over-practicality concept.

"Well," I said, "we certainly have got enough cash to get us to our next destination."

"Forty grand?" she asked.

"Yep, forty grand."

Ishi popped his head over my headrest and said, "And you are sure the gold will be safe until we return?"

I chuckled at my friend's persistence. This was the hundredth time or so that he'd brought up the subject of our gold since we survived our latest misadventure. Marie had stored almost all of it in a safe deposit box in Tegucigalpa's most prestigious industrial bank. The gold was indeed safest there. Although we missed out on the vast fortune all of us had hoped for, when added to my collection of artifacts that were also now locked safely away, none of us would have to worry about anything for many years to come.

"What have I already told you, broheim?" I asked.

Ishi shook his head while smiling sheepishly, and relaxed in his seat. Meanwhile, Marie put the Jeep in gear, chuckling to herself as she pulled us back onto the road.

"I'm gonna miss this place," I said softly.

"Hmm, me too, Nick," Ishi echoed from the back seat.

"I think you'll both love it in the Maldives," said Marie. "We should be at the airport in about twenty minutes, and then we'll be on our way within the hour. I think you'll both especially like exploring the island we'll be staying on. Beautiful beaches, crystal-clear lagoons, and a certain cave that is rumored to be home to pirate gold. Indian Ocean pirate gold."

"No shit? So, that's why we're going there?"

I must admit, my tone brightened up considerably. And, here I thought I'd have to tolerate the month or two of 'sightseeing' while planning my own excursion to Egypt to finish what Mario Thomas and I had set out to do when both of us made a pact as freshmen at UCLA sixteen years ago.

"Nick...I've grown to really like you, and I look forward to spending quality time doing the things that normal people do," said Marie. "But you will totally drive me insane if you turn into some sort of social puppy dog. You are an archaeologist. Well sort of. But, no matter where life takes us together, you'll always be you, and I would never dream of changing that. So let's see if we can dip in and out of each other's preferred worlds and keep the fire going."

"Fair enough," I said, nodding thoughtfully. Nothing like a gal who has her claws in a guy's heart, but not in his freedom to be who he is. "This just might work."

"Enough, already!" said Ishi, shaking his head. I think, perhaps, in disgust.

"Aye, matey," I said, in my finest pirate brogue, while shooting a smug smile toward him and a wink to the lady who was forging a hole in the steel wall that protects my heart. "Now let's hear what Marie has to say about this here buried treasure and some Indian Ocean pirate lore."

Sounds like fun. Stay tuned...the three of us might have another adventure to share someday.

Until then, you might avoid looking for a certain lost city of gold deep in the Honduran jungles. I'd hate to someday read about some unsuspecting traveler falling headfirst into a previously unknown burning lake of fire.

Cheers,
Nick

The End

Nick Caine returns in:

Treasure of the Deep

Available now!
eBook * Kobo * Nook
Apple * Smashwords
Paperback * Audio Book

Also available:

Plague of Coins
The Judas Chronicles #1
by Aiden James

Plague of Coins is available at:
eBook * Paperback * Audio Book

CHAPTER ONE

*T**his looks promising….*
It was late one evening, and I stood in the bowels of the Smithsonian Center for Materials Research. The staff had gone home for the night, and I was alone. Surrounded by lab equipment, computers, and stacks of dusty old books, this room could only be described as creepy. *Damned* creepy.

Then again, many would describe me as damned creepy, too. And maybe a little shady—at least if I ever get caught rummaging around in the basement. As a Smithsonian archivist, most of what I spend my days reviewing is upstairs or in other locales managed by the National Museum of History. Really, I rarely venture outside of the Anthropological Archives' scope of responsibility. Just like a good, dependable archivist should be doing.

Oh, it isn't so terrible, all cynicism aside. In my current vocation, I've been privileged to view some of the most 'secret' collections of field notes, photographs, and correspondence from the more significant scientific expeditions covering the past two centuries. Hell, that's why the job appealed to me in the first place. My son, Dr. Alistair Wolfgang Barrow, the noted historian and professor at Georgetown, is the one who brought it to my attention. Yes, he's the very same historian noted for his treatments concerning the Middle East and its volatile tensions. Tensions fueled by millennia of history and bad blood that will take decades if not centuries to cure, despite the latest diplomatic progress.

But I digress.

Upon the near-obsolete video screen, a collection of articles and photographs spanning nearly eighty years scrolled before my eyes. All of this information centered around one small village in Iran. Al-haroun is the name of the place.

I paused to sip my coffee while rubbing my eyes. Not so much from being tired as the damned viewer's fuzziness. I'm spoiled by my MAC.

Yes, very promising…could be home to one small, priceless piece of silver….

I get a feel for things, you see. It's something I've gotten better with over time. Call it honed experience, or perhaps it's the mastery that comes with practice and carefully aged wisdom and acute perception.

Okay…I can almost hear the indignant silent questions out there. 'And who in the hell are *you*, hot shot?' That's what *I'd* be wondering right about now, after re-reading the first two pages of my story.

Fair enough. My name is William. William J. Barrow, though I'm sure you already determined my last name from my son. I like the name William, actually better than any other moniker I've gone by since the Crusades ended. It makes it a lot easier for me to fit in without engendering questions about *who* I am or *where* I come from. I like it much better than any of the Apostle names like Peter, Paul, and Matthew. Although, pretending to be Bartholomew nearly two thousand years ago was a lot of fun.

That got you, I'm sure.

It would make me older than dirt. Right? Well, if we ever cross paths you won't even notice me if it's some ancient Methuselah you're seeking. I don't look a day over thirty—haven't looked a day past the 'prime of life' since I wrote my own chapter on the most famous stage in modern history.

Back then my Hebrew name was Yehuda. I guess if history had left me hanging from some tree or tripping into a garden to where my guts squirted out of my condemned body, the world would be no wiser. My role in the ultimate betrayal long forgotten, maybe I'd be just a small footnote, and not the most reviled human being ever to walk this earth.

You can thank the Greeks and Romans for that honor, unfortunately. Or, I guess I can…at least credit goes to them. Born in Kenoth in the region of Judea, and falsely accused of being a member of the 'Sicari'. Yes, these are all clues…. Give up?

The Greek for Yehuda is Yudas, and that name in Roman is Judas.

So there…that's me. I'm Judas Iscariot.

But before you simply close this book in disgust, let me explain a few things. Things that could change your mind about the above claim, and take on a little of my perspective. In truth, I could literally give a rat's ass if you believe I'm Judas or not. It's not even the reason I've decided to write down my story. After all, if I don't gain the final nine silver pieces needed for my restitution during my current 'lifetime ruse' as William Barrow, I'll still be working on this project while you and everyone you care about has died and passed away. Perhaps all of you will land in the eternal Holy Mecca I so badly long for…. To be forgiven at long last and reunited with the One I looked on as a mere prophet and wonderful teacher, instead of the Lord of Lords that He is.

How do I know the truth about Jesus now as compared to then? You'll have to read on for that answer—and it comes in bits and pieces, really. No, it won't be some pompous sermon. What I've learned these past two thousand years transcends anything and everything you've ever read in *any* book—including what is considered the standards for the Holy Scriptures—like the Bible, Koran, etc. You'd be surprised at the shenanigans I've witnessed that later became the accepted "truth from the very mouth of God Almighty."

So much is rubbish, and yet hidden within it all is the truth. Or, at least a version of the *eternal* truth.

But I digress, again. Just know that I am supremely confident of this: everyone's burning questions will be answered by the end of my story...the first installment of what remains of my earthly quest.

So, back to this place called Al-haroun. While there are many places in the world that suffer from a host of calamities, only a few originate from a small epicenter within a few square miles. And not every one of these places contains what I need. However, since at first glance it is impossible to know for sure, I must research them all.

As a town, Al-haroun is no stranger to the wrath of God, or if you will, the unfortunate reputation as a cursed place. That night, I viewed article after article, along with an endless stream of film images to support the stories—literally, an endless succession of earthquakes, floods, famines, wars, and plague. Even a rare tornado struck the town in 1942 that destroyed nine homes and killed three people. Not exactly catastrophic weather, unless you consider the fact this is Iran we're talking about and not Topeka, Kansas.

But all in all, if one considers the previous millennium's host of travesties visited upon this small area, I have to consider the likely source: a single coin. Buried somewhere, and likely hidden from the light of day for centuries. Meanwhile, hundreds, if not thousands of lives have been ruined—either killed, homeless, or both. The last article I looked at talked about a rare blizzard from thirty years ago. That event took place in May, when things begin to heat up near the Alborz Mountains. More than three feet of snow fell upon the town, and the temperatures plummeted deeply enough to destroy livestock and crops.

The people believe they're cursed, that somehow they've offended Allah. If only they knew that something there—likely buried beneath the soil—was indeed offensive to God, they might burn everything to the ground and leave. Forever.

My gut instinct was telling me a single silver shekel was responsible. One that bears Caesar's notorious beak of a nose on one side and a proud eagle upon the back. Just like twenty-nine others I once accepted as payment for my evil deed. A moment of folly, and to think it could've been forty pieces of silver if Caiaphas hadn't tried to cheat me by offering half-shekels instead.

Anyway, I was certain my assumption was one hundred percent correct. As I studied the latest stories and pictures on the screen, my left hand began to tremble. This familiar sensation always confirms the truth of what my intuitions tell me.

Silver 'blood-coin' number twenty-two is within reach.

Satisfied, I turned off the viewer. I then returned the older film to the correct cabinets and the newer CDs and flash drives to their file drawers.

It was time to request some vacation days, and make arrangements for a little trip overseas.

Also available:

Aladdin Relighted
The Aladdin Trilogy #1
by J.R. Rain
and Piers Anthony

Aladdin Relighted is available at:
eBook * Kobo * Nook
Apple * Smashwords
Paperback * Audio Book

CHAPTER ONE

She was a fine beauty with almond-shaped eyes, high cheek-bones and lips so full they could hardly close. She stepped into my tent and shook out her hair and slapped the trail dust from her overcoat.

I had been dozing lightly, one foot propped up on a heavy travel chest, when I heard a woman's voice asking for me. With my foot still hanging over the ornately-engraved chest, I had turned my head with some interest and watched as a dark-haired woman had poked her head in my open tent. My tent was always open. After all, I was always open for business. Once confirming she had the right tent, she had strode in confidently.

And that's when I sat up, blinking hard. It was not often that such a beauty entered my humble tent. Granted, there had been a time when I was surrounded by such beauties, but that seemed like a long, long time ago.

"Do you always sleep during the day?" she asked. As she spoke, she scanned my simple tent, wrinkling her nose. She stepped over to a low table and looked down at a carving of mine. She nodded to herself, as if she approved of my handiwork. She looked around my tent some more, and when she was done, she looked at me directly, perhaps challengingly.

"Only until the sun goes down."

She had been looking at a pile of my dirty robes sitting in one corner of my tent. She snapped her head around. "I hope you're joking."

"And why would you hope that?"

"Because I will not hire a sluggard."

She was a woman of considerable wealth, that much was for sure. She also did not act like any woman I had even seen, outside of the many courtyards and palaces I had once been accustomed to. She reminded me of all that was wrong with wealth and royalty and I immediately took a disliking to her, despite her great beauty.

Through my tent opening came the sounds of money being exchanged for any number of items. At the opening, swirling dust still hovered in the air from when she had entered. The dust caught some of the harsh sunlight, forming phantasmagorical shapes that looked vaguely familiar.

"And why would my lady need to hire a lazy wretch like me?" I asked. As I spoke I lifted my sandled foot off the chest and sat back with my elbows on my knees.

"Emir Farid said some satisfactory things about you. In particular, that you have proven to be somewhat reliable."

"Emir Farid has always greatly admired me."

She studied me closely. Her almond-shaped eyes didn't miss much. Her long fingers, I saw, were heavy with jewels.

"Aren't you going to offer me a seat?" she asked.

I motioned to the area in front of the chest. The area was covered in sand and didn't look much different than the desert outside my tent.

I really ought to clean this place, I thought.

"Never mind," she said. "I'll stand."

I shrugged and grinned. She fanned her face and looked around my tent some more. She didn't seem pleased, but she also looked desperate. Desperate usually won out.

She said, "Despite your many flaws, according to Emir Farid, he says that you are particularly adept at...finding things."

"I'm also adept at losing things, my lady, but funny how no one seems to want to hire me for that."

Outside, a few tents down, an animal shrieked, followed by sounds of splashing, and I knew a goat had been slaughtered. A dry, hot wind found its way into my tent, swirling the dirt at her feet, and lifting her robe around her ankles.

Nice ankles.

She caught me looking at them and leveled a withering stare at me. I grinned some more.

"You make a lot of jokes," she said. "This could be a problem."

I moved to sit back in the position she had found me in. "Then I wish you luck in your quest to find whatever it is that's missing. May I suggest you take a look around our grand market place. Perhaps this thing of which you seek is under your very nose." I closed my eyes and folded my hands over my chest.

"Are you always like this?" she demanded.

"Lying down? Often."

She made a small, frustrated noise. "Is there anyone else in this godforsaken outpost who can help me?"

"There's a shepherd who's been known to be fairly adept at finding lost goats—although, come to think of it, he did lose one last week—"

"Enough," she snapped. "I don't have much time and you will have to do, although you are older than I had hoped."

"My lady is full of compliments. I am not sure if I should blush or sleep."

"Neither, old man. Come, there's much to do."

I heard her step towards the open flap of my tent. I still hadn't opened my eyes. I lifted my hand and rested it on the corner of the chest. I hunkered deeper on the padding that doubled as my bed. She stopped at the entrance.

"Well?" she asked impatiently.

"Well what?"

"Aren't you coming?"

I turned my head and looked at her. She was standing with her hands on her hips, silhouetted in the streaming sunlight. God, she was beautiful. And irritating.

I said, "Not until I know what you want me for and we have discussed my price."

She turned and faced the bustling marketplace just outside my tent. She wanted to leave. She wanted to run. But she needed my help, that much was obvious. I waited, smiling contentedly to myself.

She said, "If I tell you on the trail, I will double your asking price."

Double was good. I jumped to my feet and grabbed a satchel and my chest. The rest could stay.

At the tent entrance, I nodded at her. "You have yourself a deal."

ABOUT THE AUTHORS

J.R. Rain is an ex-private investigator who now writes full-time in the Pacific Northwest. He lives in a small house on a small island with his small dog, Sadie, who has more energy than Robin Williams. Please visit him at www.jrrain.com.

Aiden James is a real life paranormal investigator in Tennessee. Please visit his website at: www.aidenjamesfiction.com.

Made in the USA
Monee, IL
11 January 2024

51621091R00076